THE
JOSIE
GAMBIT

———

Books by Mary Francis Shura

The Josie Gambit
The Search for Grissi
Happles and Cinnamunger
The Barkley Street Six-pack
Mister Wolf and Me
The Gray Ghosts of Taylor Ridge
The Riddle of Raven's Gulch

and the companion books
Chester
Eleanor
Jefferson

THE
JOSIE
GAMBIT

Mary Frances Shura

DODD, MEAD & COMPANY
New York

1 2 3 4 5 6 7 8 9 10

Library of Congress Cataloging-in-Publication Data

Shura, Mary Francis.
  The Josie gambit.

  Summary: Shy, twelve-year-old, chess-loving Greg is
apprehensive about spending six months with his
grandmother in Pineville, Illinois, but his relation-
ship with the outgoing Nolan family involves him in
some real-life chess moves with a troubled girl, that
open him up to loyalty and friendship with people who
really count.
  [1. Friendship—Fiction. 2. Chess—Fiction]
I. Title.
PZ7.S55983Jo 1986   [Fic]   85–31106
ISBN 0–396–08810–4

To the White Queen
from
her devoted pawn

CONTENTS

———

Part Three
THE END GAME

Part One

THE
OPENING
GAME

1

A New Beginning

TO UNDERSTAND THIS story about Josie Nolan, Tory Mitchell, and me, you have to know what the word "gambit" means. A gambit is a strategy in the game of chess. When a player gives up or sacrifices a game piece in order to get into a better position to win, that's called a gambit. The most dangerous gambit of all is a queen's gambit, because the queen is the most powerful chess piece. A gambit is a very high-risk play you shouldn't try unless you're willing to live with the way the game turns out.

When I started putting all this down, I was

only doing it for Mom. But I didn't want to send it to her until it made sense to me. So many strange things happened that I decided to write in the form of a story. I even made up a title with the word "mystery" in it. Things you don't understand are mysterious. I didn't understand, and I couldn't believe, that a twelve-year-old kid like Tory Mitchell would try a gambit in real life, risking people instead of pawns and pieces.

This all happened to me because Mom had to go to Europe on business for six months. As she wasn't going to be in any one city for more than a week, I couldn't go with her. We had never been apart that long, and it was scary to think of staying in Pineville, Illinois, with my grand-mother all that time. I think Mom was scared too, but she didn't admit it.

Instead, she gave herself away by saying the same things over and over. She must have said "I'm going to miss you" a hundred times. She must have told me "Be sure and write" a thousand times. When she left just after Christmas, nobody said much in the car on the long drive from Pine-ville to the airport. Then, when Grandma and I were waiting for her flight to be announced, Mom looked up at me with a shocked expression.

"Greg," she wailed. "This is a half a year of your growing up that I'll completely miss!"

When you're twelve and a boy and taller than most men, the last thing you want to do is bawl in an airport waiting room. I swallowed hard a couple of times and then grinned because that usually helps. "Tell you what I'll do," I said. "I'll write down everything that happens every single day."

She gave me a look of mock horror. "Play by play, like you report on your chess games?"

"Just the winning moves," I reassured her. Right then the stewardess flipped the door open and called Mom's flight number for loading. Mom grabbed my arms and gripped them hard for a minute before picking up her briefcase. I have that lady trained. She doesn't kiss me in public places unless I make the first move. But I hugged her and kissed her cheek so she knew it was okay. She looked back and pretended to grin as she disappeared into the loading tube.

I led Grandma up to where you can see the planes take off and pretended not to notice how wet her eyes were.

Pineville, Illinois. I was going to spend a whole six months in Pineville, Illinois.

2

The Ice Maiden

I WENT OVER TO SEE Josie Nolan and her family the night Mom left. Grandma insisted on my going.

It was dark by the time we got back to Pineville from the airport. I turned on the Christmas tree lights and built up the fire. Grandma kept the hard wood she bought each fall stacked in the garage. Something squeaked and scurried when I pulled logs from the pile to carry inside. Christmas had been fantastic. The hearth fire had never gone out, and Grandma kept refilling a big wooden bowl with apples she had bought from an orchard right near town. In the days Mom was there, the house was always full of her friends coming to say good-bye and welcome me to Pineville. Suddenly the same house, with the fire and the tree unchanged, felt cold and empty.

"You need to get out and around," Grandma said. "Why don't you go over to see the Nolans while I clean up this place?"

I probably need to explain Grandma. No matter what she has on, it looks like a sweater and skirt. Everything about her is efficient—short hair she doesn't have to mess with, a streak of lipstick put on without a mirror, and one earring, always in her right ear. Librarians answer the phone a lot and take the left earring off because it hurts. And she's not the sort of person you can talk out of things.

When I hesitated, she grinned at me. "Shoo! Get out. I've got work to do."

I've lived just outside of Washington, D. C., ever since I can remember. Virginia's winters aren't anything to build igloos against. Illinois takes its seasons seriously. Talk about a white Christmas! I walked over toward the Nolan house through drifts that rolled on as far as I could see, studded by drooping trees. Every bush was a rounded hump, and lazy smoke wavered white against a pale sky.

When Mom and I first talked about my staying with Grandma, I tried to remember what Pineville was like. But, other than Grandma's, I could only bring back the Nolan house with its wide front porch, the giant horse chestnut tree in back with the wonderful tree house, and Mr. Nolan leaning over the chessboard in the front room. He wasn't any kin to me but, like everybody in town, I called him Grandpa Nolan. He lived there with his son, who was married and had three children, one of them Josie. Grandpa Nolan had taught chess so long that he had championship students all over the State of Illinois. I knew the Nolan family better than I did anyone else in town. Some of Mom's old chums had kids my age but none of them lived close enough to make friends with when I'd only been there during Mom's brief vacations.

I was that kind of little kid who didn't have many close friends anyway. I guess I've always been shy. I always read a lot and didn't mind being by myself. People buy games for kids like that. Mom bought me a chess set the Christmas

I was six. When I got really excited about it, Grandma took me over to meet Grandpa Nolan so he could help me get started right. After that, every time we went back to Pineville, I played with him.

There was a Nolan boy four years older than I named Jason, and a little blonde kid they called Lollie, besides Josie, who was my age. Josie was the only girl who had ever beaten me at chess three times running. Often since then, when I won a big match, I'd wondered if Josie could still beat me. Over the last three years, Grandma had come to Virginia to visit us. She had told me when Grandpa Nolan died. Josie might even have quit playing, for all I knew.

One thing about Pineville, you don't feel edgy about walking around at night by yourself. The streets were quiet, with only an occasional car scrunching nervously along. I figured I would just walk a while and then go back to Grandma's. Nobody knows how shy I am but Mom, and she's a good sport and doesn't talk about it.

Then I walked past the Nolan house.

To be honest, I passed it two or three times. The porch light was on and a faint glow shone through the closed drapes. Smoke wavered out of the chimney, bluish and smelling of woods in autumn. I wondered if the Nolans had mice in their woodpile too, like Grandma did.

Finally I got up the courage to ring the doorbell.

I rang twice and was about to go away when the door opened. Josie Nolan had really changed in the three years since I'd last seen her. She had been a sort of chunky kid at nine. This Josie Nolan was as tall as any girl in my class back home. She looked downright skinny in tight-legged, faded jeans and a sweat shirt. I remembered her hair as a sort of liver-colored brown, but under the hall light it was as much red as it was brown—auburn I guess that is—and shiny. She was pretty in that kind of low-key way I can handle—dark eyes and a smooth skin without a lot of makeup on.

She smiled at once. "Greg," she said, in a really pleased tone, and opened the door wider for me to come in.

Then I saw she had company. Another girl was looking up at me curiously from the rug in front of the fire. She was wearing a bright blue sweater and a white skirt that fanned out on the floor around her. I couldn't believe anyone could be that pretty. Pale curls framed her face, and her eyes were the clearest, coldest blue I've ever seen.

"I guess I should have called," I began. "I mean, I was just walking by. Please don't let me bother . . ."

Josie chuckled. "We had all begun to wonder when you were going to get yourself over here." Then she turned. "Greg Farrell, this is my friend Tory Mitchell. Come on in, you're freezing us out." She took my jacket and hung it on the hall tree. "You've grown, but I guess we all have. Wait until you see my brother Jason. He's immense, too. Come on in and sit down."

I was hanging back on purpose. "Listen, Josie," I said. "I didn't think about your having company. I don't want to break in on anything."

She shook her head. "Tory and I were just sitting here talking. Come on. We're glad for a distraction, aren't we, Tory?"

She had kept raising her voice as she talked, just so I could hear her. She had to. The minute I'd stepped inside the door, a low-slung, hairy dog had come flying out from the back of the house, barking like fury. She made so much noise that my ears vibrated.

Tory Mitchell didn't even try to fight the noise. She watched me silently without even nodding at my greeting. Maybe girls that pretty didn't feel they had to be polite.

I bent down and offered the dog my hand to smell, just the way I'd been taught.

Josie grabbed my arm and pushed it back against my chest. "No, no," she told me urgently. "Miss Pod bites."

I looked at the dog again. This creature with her top hair pulled up in a bow weighed all of fifteen pounds, dripping wet. She had that kind of dished face that reminds you of a stuffed toy and the most immense, soft brown eyes I had ever seen.

"*That* bites?" I asked, smiling at the idea of a ferocious guard dog wearing a red satin ribbon on top of her head.

"She's usually good for fourteen stitches," Josie said, almost proudly. "She's a Llaso Apso. That's Tibetan for a man-eating mop. The mailman calls her Miss Ferocity of the Western World."

Josie started into the living room. "Just don't sit down anywhere until I've checked for biscuits," she warned me.

I watched her make a brisk search of the

furniture. She pulled up the pillows on the couch and chairs and felt beneath them. Apparently she didn't find any biscuits because she waved for me to come over by the fire.

All this time, Tory Mitchell was sitting very straight without saying a word, just watching us both with her eyes narrowed a little. Strange, I decided. Or maybe she was as shy as I was about talking to strangers.

"Miss Pod is very defensive about her food," Josie explained. "She hides her dog biscuits to keep us from taking them back. Then she attacks anyone who sits down where she has them hidden. There," she went on. "Take the chair by the fire."

I looked at the dog and she looked back at me. I knew my expression was friendlier than hers. She had finally quit barking but I had the feeling I was only on probation.

Then I glanced over at Tory Mitchell. I looked away again quickly. There's something spooky about someone who stares silently at you like that. Her face was perfectly shaped and just beautiful. I had never seen such a pretty girl my own age. But with her lips held together and her cold eyes on me, I decided her expression was even more threatening than Miss Pod's.

3

Ogres and Ghosts

AS I CROSSED THE living room, I glanced toward the corner where I had played chess with Grandpa Nolan. The hassock we'd used was just where it had always been. Boy, did that corner bring back memories. Grandpa Nolan must have taught a hundred people to play chess. I was just lucky to be one of them. He never became a champion himself, but lots of the people he taught went on to win matches everywhere. I used to imagine how it would feel when I won a world championship and could come back to Pineville and tell Grandpa Nolan about it. When he died, that dream died with him.

Every time we'd played, I'd get to set out Grandpa Nolan's chessmen. There are dozens of styles in chessmen, but most serious chess players prefer a Staunton set. Howard Staunton was an English scholar who was the best player in England and maybe the world for thirty years. Staunton chessmen are very plain. They are gracefully shaped, and it is easy to tell one piece from another when they are all mixed up out on the board. Grandpa Nolan's carved wooden Staunton set fitted into a box lined with green felt. The pieces were smooth, almost satiny to the touch, from all those years in his hands.

When I realized Josie was watching me, I turned and went over by the fire. She had to feel the same way I did about that chess corner. She'd sat there with him a lot more hours than I had.

I waited until Josie plumped down on the rug beside Tory Mitchell before taking the chair by the fire. "How is everybody?" I asked her.

Grandpa Nolan had teased a lot with words. Josie grinned up at me and answered in the same kidding style. "It's easy enough to tell you about us," she said. "Just pick a letter! Take *A*. Jason is adolescent, I am aspiring, Lollie is adorable. How about *O*? Overwhelming, odd, obnoxious."

When I laughed, she shook her head soberly. "Believe me, the Nolans have things sorted out. Jason got the athletic talent, Lollie has the looks. I have the Game of Kings." She glanced up at me as she said this, knowing I would remember Grandpa Nolan's calling chess that.

Tory finally quit watching me and turned toward the fire. She looped her arms around her legs and stared into the glowing bed of coals. Josie glanced at her once in a while in a concerned way. I felt sorry for Josie, but what could she do when someone was acting so strange and rude?

Miss Pod had been studying me soberly this whole time. She suddenly granted royal approval in her own individual style. Gathering herself into a catapult, she literally shot through the air and landed in my lap, her long hair flying.

You have to remember that Mom and I always lived in an apartment back in Virginia. Since no pets were allowed in our building, I only saw dogs on leashes and at dog shows. I'd never had one perched on my lap, staring at me with eyes that were not really round at all but a little squared at the corners.

I must have gasped when she landed, but

then I sat very still while she wriggled herself into a comfortable dog tuffet and twisted her head around to stare up into my face.

"Be careful with your hands," Josie warned me. "Miss Pod makes friends by degrees. Only touch her behind the ears."

Holding that dog was like having a warm hairy hand grenade on my lap. I scratched Miss Pod behind the ears carefully and grinned at Josie.

"See?" she asked. "You're making progress." As she spoke, a frantic wail came from upstairs. Josie was on her feet in one swift motion. As she raced through the hall, she called back, "You remember Lollie. She has nightmares about ogres and ghosts. I'll be right back."

Miss Pod twisted her head to watch her go. I felt her muscles tense. I really expected her to take off after Josie. Instead, she relaxed and settled back to staring at me. The minute Josie disappeared at the top of the stairs, Tory turned those cold blue eyes on me.

"What are you doing here, anyway?"

I could feel my face get red. Did she mean here in the Nolan house or in Pineville? "Grandpa Nolan taught me to play chess a long time ago," I told her. "I always come here when I'm in town."

"So when are you going back to wherever you came from?" She sounded as if I couldn't get going quick enough to please her.

"I'm going to stay for six months."

She frowned. "That means you'll go to school here. How come you have to be here?"

I know a lot of guys who would have put her down hard right about then, but I'm not like that and she seemed to know it. The best I could do was make my reply as cold and brief as I could. "My mother's going to be out of the country with her job and I'm staying with my grandmother."

"I wouldn't stay with my grandparents if they forced me. I hate them. I'd run away and they could just look for me till the end of time." Tory turned back to the fire. "I love my dad, but his folks are the pits. They live on a big ranch in Texas with horses and all the money in the world and snap at me about my manners every time I open my mouth." She looked over her shoulder at me. "So where's your dad?"

I hate it when people ask me that. "He died in service."

She stared at me for a minute, then got up

and straightened her skirt. "I've heard about you, you know. Everybody has. You're supposed to be the greatest kid chess player in the whole world—smart, wonderful, all that stuff. Your grandmother blats about you all the time. But she never said you were a freak. Only a freak is a mile high with beaver teeth like yours."

I stared at her, not believing what I was hearing. I had heard rude remarks before, but this girl was in a class by herself. This little ice maiden was out to draw blood, and she didn't even know me!

Before my shock waves stopped, Tory went to the hall closet for her wraps. Her jacket was some kind of white leather with a fur-trimmed hood that framed her face. How could anybody be so mean and look so fantastic? She pulled on mittens that matched the jacket and walked out the door without even saying good-bye.

A log fell in the fire and I whistled softly.

I'm that kind of a twelve-year-old boy who has had to carry his birth certificate to the movies since about the third grade to get in at the kid's price. Mom has pictures of my dad taken in uniform with a little peaked hat on top and some kind of boots laced to mid-calf with his pants blousing over. He looks tall like me and skinny as a rail. I take after him. I hit five feet by the time I was eight, and am pushing six feet at twelve. At this rate I will be able to paint roofs without a ladder by the time I am twenty.

I know I am too shy and too tall and haven't grown into my teeth yet. I know most people are only interested in a big, tongue-tied kid like me if he plays basketball. Knowing all this and having somebody say it like that to your face are two very different things.

I wanted to be back in Virginia. I wanted to be anyplace in the whole wide world but where I was. Yet Miss Pod had looked up at me when I whistled, and was thumping me with her plume of a tail.

In order to get my mind off Tory, I scratched Miss Pod's ears and thought over what Josie had said about this funny little square-eyed dog. After a minute I couldn't stand it. I eased Miss Pod off my lap and found a dictionary in the built-in bookcase beside the fireplace. Maybe Mom and I are boringly normal, but neither of us has nightmares about ogres and ghosts or defines a word in the form of a joke.

Llaso Apso is *not* the Tibetan word for "man-eating mop"; it means "curly-haired goat."

"Goat," I repeated aloud to Miss Pod. She stared at me with those big eyes and wagged her tail some more. I was glad she wasn't insulted, because I hadn't meant it that way. I sat back down and patted my lap with my hand. She landed lightly just like the other time and stared at me as steadily as Tory had until Josie came back downstairs.

Josie paused on the bottom step with a frown. "Where's Tory?" she asked.

"She went home," I told her. "I mean, I guess she did. She just got up, put on her jacket, and went out."

"She didn't say anything?"

I hesitated a moment before shaking my head. "Not about where she was going," I said.

Josie sighed and walked to the door to look out. "Maybe she'll be back right away."

Her hopeful tone made me curious. "Does she live a long way away?"

Josie came back by the fire. "Just down at the corner, but she was supposed to stay here until her mother came home."

"Is she always that quiet?" I asked. I chose the word carefully. After all, Tory hadn't said a word before Josie went upstairs.

She looked at me and grinned. "Three points

for being super tactful. Tory was just plain rude to you and I'm really sorry. But she is having a tough time."

I thought to myself that Josie didn't know the half of it.

"She really *is* having it tough," Josie went on as if she had read my mind. "She's been my best friend for more than two years now, but she's only acted like this lately. She's really a great girl and tons of fun. She's a wonderful chess player, too. She's just not herself now."

I wanted to tell her she didn't have to sell her friend to me. I already had my own opinion, thank you. One of the hard problems you have when you're not a big talker is that people decide what you're thinking and then argue about it with you. And Josie was plainly worried about her friend. She glanced at the door hopefully every few minutes.

"I can't figure what is taking her so long to get back," she said.

"Maybe she doesn't plan to come back," I suggested.

Her eyes widened as she looked at me. "Oh, but she has to! Tory told her father a lot of stuff about her mother that wasn't true, hoping to get the custody changed. Among other things, she said she was left alone a lot and was really scared. Now every time her mother leaves the house, she has to make arrangements for Tory. Tonight Tory was supposed to stay over here with me."

I grinned to myself, thinking how much time I have always spent alone when Mom was working, but I didn't say anything. Josie got up and looked at me hesitantly. "Do you mind if I make a phone call? Just to see that Tory is all right?"

She dialed the number, waited, and then dialed again several times before coming back to the living room. "I can't get anything but a busy signal," she said, frowning a little. "I guess I just have to figure she's all right."

I wanted to tell her that in my opinion Tory would take care of herself no matter what happened to anyone else. I only nodded.

4

The Chess Team

IT MAY SEEM AS IF I am going on endlessly about that first evening at the Nolans. But that evening became important to my story because of how it came to an end. Tory didn't come back, and Josie was restless. About the third time she got up to go look out into the street, she sighed. "I'm driving myself crazy and that's ridiculous! Come on to the kitchen with me."

The Nolan kitchen is a huge, square room with cupboards all around and a door leading to a pantry that's bigger than any of the clothes closets in our apartment back home. A trestle table sits right in the middle of the kitchen with chairs tucked under. Josie pulled out a chair for me and started to fix us popcorn.

Instead of doing it the way it tells you to on the jar or using a popper, Josie just poured oil into a big copper-bottomed pan, dumped in popcorn, and put the lid on.

"I've never seen anybody make it like that," I told her.

"Jason's invention," she said. "If you let the popcorn warm up and jump to the top with just a shake now and then, it almost tends to itself and you never get those burned spots on the pans." She paused and frowned. "Well, almost never," she amended. While the oil sizzled, she fixed cold Cokes for both of us and put a small pan of butter to melt on a back burner.

"What did you do about your sister's nightmare?" I asked her. "She sure shut up fast."

Josie shrugged and grinned. "It's a breeze. You flip on the light and do an Ogre and Ghost Search by looking everywhere they could hide. There was some Christmas tissue under her bed that looked to her like a ghost. By the time I found it, she was already half asleep."

The popcorn had begun to explode in the

pan. She shook it with one hand while she reached for a huge pottery bowl. In no time at all, it was salted and buttered and we were back in front of the fire.

Before she set the bowl down, she went to the window again and looked out into the street. Neither of us was having very much luck forgetting about Tory Mitchell.

"Tell me why you didn't get to go to Europe with your Mom. I'd love to go over there."

"I would, too," I told her. "Maybe some other time I can. But this trip Mom isn't going to be any one place long enough for me to go to school and finish this year. It was a hard decision for both of us."

She nodded thoughtfully.

The minute Josie set the popcorn down, Miss Pod had posted herself directly in front of her chair. Sitting up on her hind legs, she frantically waved both paws in the air. She looked for all the world as if she were running a pump. She didn't make a sound, just pawed the air and stared at Josie. Every few words, Josie picked out a piece of popcorn and handed it to her. When Miss Pod had it in her mouth, she'd turn and glare at me, growling fiercely.

"What's that all about?"

"I told you she was defensive about food," Josie reminded me. "That's to warn you not to try to take it away from her."

"Be my guest," I told Miss Pod. Maybe all those dogs on leashes in the park back in Arlington were as crazy as this one. I doubted it very much.

"Then you'll be going to my school?" Josie asked.

I nodded. When she didn't say anything more, I asked her how it was.

She cocked her head to think about that. Then she laughed quietly. "How can I say? I haven't anything to compare it with."

I stared into the fire, realizing for the first time how much I dreaded starting in at a new school.

"It must be tough to switch like that," Josie said, handing the dog another kernel of corn. "Leaving all your friends and all."

I tightened my shoulders. "I've never been all that great at making friends. But I'll miss Washington. You never run out of new things to see there. And I'll miss the other kids on the team."

"Team," she repeated, frowning. "I should have thought of that. You probably play basketball like Jason does."

I shook my head. "I'm on the chess team." I didn't tell her I had been captain for two years or played the top slot, though I thought about it.

She stared at me. "Greg!" she said, suddenly excited. "You'll go to *our* school! You could be in *our* chess club!"

Josie explained that she and the other kids in the school who played chess had talked themselves blue to get a club started in the first place. The problem was a sponsor. The Latin teacher sponsored the Latin Club, an English teacher sponsored the Writers' Circle, and so forth. Since nobody taught chess and none of the teachers played it, no one had wanted to be sponsor.

"We finally talked Miss Ryan, one of the music teachers, into being our sponsor. She's only doing it because she's neat. She sits there during meetings and knits Aran Island sweaters while we play. When an argument comes up, she hands us the rule book."

I laughed, remembering our chess coach back home. Mr. Micek never opened a rule book. Instead, he showed us how a similar problem had been solved in some world-famous match.

"I'd like to join your chess club," I admitted. "It sounds great."

"There's more," Josie said. Miss Pod had gotten tired of begging and whined for her next piece of popcorn. "Last fall one of the other junior highs, way on the other side of town, challenged us to a series of matches this spring. Our principal went all to pieces.

" 'We can't do that,' he told us. 'You don't even have a coach. It's one thing for you kids just to play, but we could make a dreadful showing and disgrace the entire school.' " Josie grinned at me.

"I know about your winning matches back East because your grandmother tells everybody who comes into the library. With you playing for us, we couldn't possibly make a dreadful showing. Grandpa said you were a natural."

I looked at her doubtfully. Maybe the team *could* make a dreadful showing. I knew I could if I froze up. Back home I'd had all the rest of the team silently rooting for me. It might not be that way here in Pineville.

"The matches start in February. We are going to play off for team positions as soon as school starts up. We only get to send three players to a match. Come on, Greg!"

I whistled softly. "Only three players? But you must already have more than that. Surely you're one."

"I'm at the bottom," she admitted cheerfully. "I taught Tory how to play and now she beats me four times out of five. Come on. Say you'll at least try out?"

Without meaning to, I looked back over to where Grandpa Nolan's chair sat in the half darkness beyond the lamplight. "If you think I should."

"No question," she said firmly. She got up and looked out into the snowy street again before coming back with a chessboard. It wasn't Grandpa Nolan's board, which was inlaid with two kinds of wood. This was an ordinary cardboard one that showed a lot of wear. Without even asking me, she took down a box of chessmen and picked out two pawns. With a black pawn in one hand and a white pawn in the other, she held her fists out to me so I couldn't see which was which.

I grinned and tapped the back of her left

hand. She turned it over and opened it to reveal the white pawn.

"See?" she said eagerly. "You get the first turn. That's an omen. You'll make the team. Come on, let's set up."

5

Late Alarms

SINCE I GOT TO MAKE the debut—the opening
move—it took me a minute to decide which one
to use. I had learned a lot about openings since
I last played with Josie. I decided to use Grandpa
Nolan's favorite because I knew Josie would be
comfortable with it.

She had learned more about the game, too.
I could tell from the tense way she watched me
through the first few moves. Then she looked
at me and grinned.

One thing about Josie. She comes right out
with what she thinks. "Whew," she said after a
few minutes. "I was scared to death you were

going to pull some new fancy trick on me." She lifted a strand of hair out of her face and moved her piece. "I wanted you to be good enough to make the team, but I didn't want you to wipe me out first thing."

Halfway through the game, I called Grandma so she wouldn't be walking the floor.

That evening was fun. I would have had more fun if Josie had been able to forget about Tory Mitchell. When she went to the phone to call her again and only got a busy signal, I really felt bad.

"I think it's my fault your friend went away," I told her. "She didn't like me."

Josie stared at me. "What is there not to like about you?"

I could have given her Tory's list but I didn't. "Maybe she felt I was in the way."

Josie made a really dumb move. She simply didn't have her mind on what she was doing. "More likely she just didn't want to be here," she said in a worried tone. "I sure hope she gets off her high horse before next month. She's supposed to spend a whole week with us while her mom takes some training program in Minneapolis."

I didn't mean to stare at her like that, but

there was so much hurt in her voice I wanted to tell her Tory Mitchell wasn't worth being unhappy about.

She glanced up at me and laughed. "I recognize that expression on your face," she said. "You're getting ready to make a really crafty move. Grandpa Nolan got that very same look when he was ready to put me into checkmate."

Would it be polite to disappoint a hostess? I shrugged and did it.

She was a good sport. She had already started setting the pieces up for another game when a siren began to scream outside, sounding as close as the front porch. Colored lights flashed wildly across the snowy windows, shining through the icicles hanging from the eaves. Horns blared from all directions. Naturally Miss Pod went wild, hurling herself against the door and barking like crazy.

Without benefit of ogres and giants, Josie's little sister Lollie woke up and started wailing. Josie shot up the stairs two at a time, while I went to the front door to look outside.

It's awful to say something like that is pretty, but it really was. The red and blue lights on top of the squad cars were still flashing and they spun through the falling snow. They cut bands of radiance like ribbons clear into the icy limbs of the big trees on the other side of the street. People were gathered in dark knots even in front of the Nolan house, so that it took me a minute to realize that the police cars—there were two of them—were down at the corner where Tory lived, along with this big dark limousine like you see on Embassy Row in Washington, D.C.

The whole scene was confusing. The sidewalk was crowded with people dressed in regular clothes, as well as cops in uniform. One woman had a storm coat pulled over a long nightgown. I guessed she was a neighbor who had already gone to bed. A station wagon was parked in behind the second police car. I saw a flash of white as two policemen almost carried someone to the station-wagon door. Tory had left wearing a white jacket.

But why would policemen be hauling Tory along like that and stuffing her into a car? I was still trying to sort it out in my mind when the rest of the Nolan family came in through the back door from the garage.

"Greg!" Josie's mother cried. "Greg Farrell. You sure picked an exciting time to come." She didn't wait for me to make the first move, she just hugged me, while Josie's father shook my hand.

"What's going on out there?" I asked.

Jason started to say something but Josie came flying down the stairs, rubbing a big wet place on her sweat shirt where Lollie had cried down her front.

"Tory never came over here?" Mrs. Nolan asked Josie.

"She was here but she left." Josie came to the window beside me. "What's all the excitement about? What's going on with the police cars?"

Jason started to answer Josie's question but Mrs. Nolan put her hand on his arm. "Some kind of disturbance down the block," she said soothingly. "It's over now. One of the cars is already leaving."

"But it looked like they were at Tory's house," Josie protested, pressing her forehead against the glass to see better. I almost blurted out what I thought I had seen but Jason spoke too fast.

"That's exactly where they were," Jason said sulkily.

Josie turned to him. "But why? What's wrong?"

Mrs. Nolan gave Jason one of those "Silence or Die" looks that every kid understands, and he turned away.

Then Mrs. Nolan tried to change the subject back to me. Josie wasn't having any of that. "Tory's my friend," Josie cried. "Tell me what's wrong!"

"Now, Josie," her mother began.

Josie didn't even let her finish. She opened the door and ran out into the snow in just that sweater and her skinny jeans. The limousine was still there, but the station wagon was gone and the second police car was pulling away. The neighbors had gone back indoors.

"I'd probably better get back to Grandma's," I told Mrs. Nolan.

"Come see us," she said. "Tomorrow, early. Your grandmother will be at work and I'm dying to hear what your mom is up to in Europe."

Jason nodded. "Yeah, Farrell, come on over." He looked at me thoughtfully. "I got something I want to talk to you about."

Josie was still standing in the snow, staring down toward the apartment house where Tory lived.

"Thanks for a really good time," I told her.

She didn't look around. "That's okay, Greg,"

she said vaguely. Then she turned to me. "What happened down there, Greg? What did you see?"

She looked both scared and worried. I felt awful. If I had been sure of what I'd seen I would have told her, but I wasn't. It had been too confusing with all those flashing lights. I shook my head. "It didn't make any sense to me," I said finally.

She looked at me a long moment before glancing back toward the corner. I felt worse. But all I had really seen was somebody in white being hustled into a station wagon by the police. I had no way of knowing if it was Tory Mitchell.

Even so, I kicked snow all the way home, mad at myself because Josie had looked so bleak when she turned away.

6

Offensive Strategy

GRANDMA WAS IN BED when I got home. The note stuck on the refrigerator was quick and to the point:

"Hope you had fun. See you at breakfast."

I was glad she wasn't up. My head was too full of that evening to talk about it. I still couldn't believe Tory Mitchell. Why would anybody attack a total stranger the way she had hit out at me? Then there was that business about the cops pushing somebody into a station wagon. And it didn't seem to make sense for Mrs. Nolan to work so hard to keep Josie from knowing what was going on.

47

Very mysterious, but not enough to keep me awake.

That next morning, Grandma had my breakfast ready to serve and was reading a book when I came downstairs.

She smiled and filled my orange juice glass. She has great glasses, with an orange on the side, but they only hold three swallows. She had cooked me two slices of bacon, one egg over easy, and two pieces of toast. My mouth thought everything was delicious. My stomach didn't notice that anything had happened at all.

But she was smiling at me. "You can't imagine how great it is to see you put down a good hearty breakfast like that, Greg. I really love feeding you."

I smiled a little weakly, the way you do when you are quietly starving.

When she asked me how the Nolans were, I told her about the chess club.

"That will be something you can tell your mom in your Sunday letter."

"Sunday letter?" I asked, grinning. "Do I detect a broad hint?"

"Well, maybe." She smiled. "Your mom always wrote me a Sunday letter when she was away at college. I know how much I liked them."

"It's not the world's worst idea," I said. "After the holidays, there's going to be a chess tournament between schools. I didn't even know this town had two junior high schools."

She laughed. "It hasn't always had. But Pineville spread out a lot since your mom grew up here. An old-timer like me can get lost in those new subdivisions out west of town. They even have a shopping mall out there. There's been some talk about putting in a branch library. I hope you gave my best to the Nolans."

"I did," I told her. "And I'm going back over there today. Jason said he has something he wants to talk to me about."

"That's wonderful," she said. "I was afraid you'd be bored to death here by yourself until school started." She got up and cleared the table in a few efficient motions. As she went for her coat, she called back, "I'm running a little late this morning. I left you a sandwich in the frig. You know where the apples are. Cookies in the jar there. Eat lunch whenever you get hungry."

She had suggested it, not me. I ate the lunch before I went over to the Nolans. It was delicious. Maybe I would have saved it if I had known that

49

Jason was having his breakfast and Mrs. Nolan would insist I have pancakes too.

Mrs. Nolan had just handed me a plate of pancakes with bacon tucked in between the top and second layer when Josie came in. Miss Pod, who followed her, seemed to remember me. She came over by my chair, reared up on her tail, and began pawing the air the way she had the night before with the popcorn.

"She wants bacon," Jason told me. "Feed her at your own risk."

I grinned at Josie, self-conscious about having left in the middle of the night and being back there before she was up.

"Second breakfast," I told her. "Your mom is really persuasive."

"Persuasive is too big a word to use before breakfast," she replied, sitting down and reaching for the juice pitcher. I must have been embarrassed because a bite of pancake stalled in my throat, so that I had to swallow a lot of times before it went down.

"Using big words comes from living with grown-ups," Mrs. Nolan said. "I like it. Needing a second breakfast also comes from being with grandparents," she added. "I used to starve at my grandmother's house. Older people forget how much kids eat."

"There's always food here," Jason said, refilling his milk glass. "Just come over any time. Not always the greatest," he added with a teasing glance at his mother, "but filling."

Josie was looking at me and Jason. "I can't believe how nice he's treating you," she said. "He's made a life work of sneering at my friends."

"Selected friends," Jason corrected her. "Anyway, Greg isn't your friend, he's a family friend because of Grandpa."

Just then the doorbell rang and Miss Pod tore into the hall to protect her territory. Josie rose and followed her to the door. From where I was sitting, I could see Tory Mitchell in the doorway. She was wearing a different jacket. This time it was bright blue. Her hat was trimmed with white fur that stood out all around her face. Her mittens were the same fur. I couldn't believe I could still think she was pretty after the way she had talked to me. That business about "Pretty is as pretty does" is a lot of bunk.

"Come on in," I heard Josie say. "We're having late breakfast."

Tory looked past Josie toward us and raised

her eyebrows. "Well." She hesitated. "Just for a minute. But I don't want anything to eat. I only came to say good-bye."

It wasn't that anyone meant to eavesdrop, but the hall is just off the kitchen and Tory wasn't trying to keep her voice down.

"Good-bye?" Josie asked in this funny voice. "What do you mean?"

"I mean we are leaving this awful neighborhood," Tory said. "I can't believe such a crummy place."

"But you live here, too," Josie reminded her. "All that business last night with the police was in your building, not at my house. Whatever it was."

I heard Jason mutter something as he scraped his chair back and started to rise. His mother laid her hand on his shoulder and pressed him down. He sighed heavily but obeyed.

"I *did* live there," Tory was saying. "That's what I came by to tell you. My mother has movers working right now, packing up our things."

Josie was silent a minute. "I don't understand all this."

Tory shook her head. "We are making a temporary move. We just can't live here any more. We'll stay with some friends of my mother's on the west side of town for a while."

"Then you'll be changing schools!" Josie asked.

"What makes you think that?" Tory challenged her.

"Now come on, Tory," Josie protested. "You know people who live out that way go to the new junior high."

"I'll commute by cab," she said. "You don't have to change schools unless a move is permanent. I would have told you last night but I didn't want to interrupt you two."

Josie flushed and turned toward us. "Greg and I kept expecting you to come back."

Tory Mitchell met my eyes across the room, her expression coldly superior. "I know better than to intrude." Then she turned back to Josie as if I had melted away. "So what did you do after I left last night?"

Josie glanced back at me, embarrassed by Tory's rudeness. Right then I would have given about one million dollars to have been that same number of miles away. "Played chess," Josie told her defensively.

Tory smiled in a really ugly way. "Sure, Josie."

Jason, beside me, let out a strangled squawk

and glared at his mother. That was even too much for her. "Listen, Tory," she began quietly.

Tory didn't give her a chance. "I apologize, Mrs. Nolan, I really do," she said smoothly. "I was just so startled. I've never thought of Josie as the kind of girl who would entertain a boy when she was supposed to be baby-sitting. I apologize, I really do."

Jason was still making furious noises. I wished I could have felt mad. Instead, I felt humiliated.

Twelve seems to be the year when a lot of people hurl themselves into the boy and girl thing. I am not ready. I mean, I am *really* not ready. But it's everywhere at school. Somebody is always whispering or giggling or being shocked or telling some crazy story about what happened at a pizza joint after a movie. Two of the girls in my class back home claimed to be going steady and wore stuff on chains to prove it. I am not ready for that. There are people I like and people I don't like, but not that way. Yet.

Very quickly, before even Mrs. Nolan could respond to her words, Tory went on. "Anyway, good-bye. It was just awful here last night and that's why we're leaving. We don't want to live in a neighborhood like this any more. I told my mother I'm not even coming back over here to stay while she goes on that silly trip of hers."

"But, Tory!" Josie protested.

"I don't want to talk about it. I just came to say good-bye. I'll see you at school."

She let herself out, with Josie staring after her.

"I'm going to be sick," Jason roared, getting up to look out the window. A rented truck was parked at the corner and men in knitted hats were carrying furniture up a ramp and storing it inside.

Josie didn't come back to the kitchen. When I heard her running up the stairs with Miss Pod clicking along behind her, I was sure Tory Mitchell would never look that pretty to me again.

Right away the movers closed the back of the truck and Tory and her mother got into a station wagon and drove away. The whole back end was piled with more stuff.

I did a real double-take. Station wagon! This one was a dark red with wooden panels. I hadn't seen the color of the one the policemen had pushed the "person in white" into. If it had been Tory, why would the police have so much trouble getting her into her own mother's car?

"Mom," Jason wailed, returning from the window. "Why do you let that little monster get away with junk like that?"

Mrs. Nolan sighed. "She is Josie's friend, Jason. She also has more problems than she can handle."

"She doesn't *have* problems, she *is* one. Why does she have to take everything out on Josie? You're not going to keep her here while her mom is away after that crack!"

Mrs. Nolan sat down across from us. "Forgive us all this, Greg. Tory is going through a bad time, and giving one to Josie. The difference is that Josie has us. Tory hasn't anybody."

"What about her mom?" Jason challenged. "What about that perfect father she's so nuts about? What about her grandparents down in Texas who wrap her in furs and designer jeans?"

"Never mind those other people," Mrs. Nolan told him in a tired tone. "Tory's mother has custody. Her new job will make it possible for her to support the child. We're keeping Tory here to help her mother, not Tory."

"Surely they can farm her out someplace," Jason said.

"Someplace isn't good enough," his mother

told him. "Her grandparents from Texas are panting for an excuse to upset that custody decision."

"If she were mine, I'd send her to them by express mail," Jason grumbled. He scraped to his feet. "Come on, Greg, I'll show you my room."

I should have known what was on Jason's mind. As soon as we got to his room, which was wall-to-wall sport posters, he waved me into his desk chair. I decided all the Nolans are very direct.

"How come you don't play basketball?"

"I don't know how, and I wouldn't be any good."

"Did you ever try?"

I nodded. "When I was eight or nine. I fell all over myself when I tried to run."

"So did I. All kids are awkward when they are really growing fast. Don't you figure you're about through growing now?"

I shrugged. "It would sure be all right with me to stop here."

"I'd work with you if you wanted to play," he said.

I stared at him. "Why would you do that? I won't be around after this year."

He shrugged. "You'll be somewhere. There's

a lot of strategy in sports, just like there is in chess. I think you'd be a winner. You might even like it."

I thought about it. This was a new idea, but maybe he was right. Maybe I could learn to play. In that silence, I heard the painful rhythm of somebody crying.

Jason heard it, too. He growled and slammed his fist into his pillow. "That's Josie. I don't know what she sees in that Tory Mitchell. But what Mom said about those people wanting custody is fascinating. Tory is always going on about how she hates her dad's parents down in Texas. From what she says, they make her act like a human being. A tall order for that kid! She has always told Josie that she intends to live with her father no matter what the court says. Maybe she's trying to be so hateful that her own mother will pitch her out."

"Where's her father in all this?"

Jason shrugged. "Who knows? All we hear is Tory's side. She couldn't define truth with an unabridged dictionary."

We talked a little more about basketball and Jason told me about the team. After a while we heard Josie going back downstairs, with the click of Miss Pod's toenails on the treads behind her.

I never knew a morning to go that fast. Jason and I fooled around in his room a while and then went outside, where I helped him shovel the walk. The next thing I knew, Mrs. Nolan was calling us for lunch. I should have insisted on going home but I never knew chili could smell that good in my life.

And it tasted as good as it smelled.

Big bowls!

7

"Dear Wandering Mom"

ALL MY LIFE I'VE heard about artists and writers starving in attics. Then, the very first time I tried writing, I found myself sleeping in a room with a pitched ceiling, starving to death.

Destiny.

Grandma's idea of writing a letter to Mom every Sunday sounded great. Maybe I could even kill two birds with one postage stamp. I could explain to Mom about this story and do something about my hollow stomach at the same time. I am including my first Sunday letter because nothing else happened that day for me to write down.

Dear Mom,

This is my first Sunday here, and here is your first Sunday letter. I want to warn you right off that I am including a sort of puzzle in this letter. Don't feel bad if you can't solve it because I'm going to give you the answer anyway. My life could depend on it!

Grandma's fine and really fun to talk to because she's interested in everything and knows how to listen.

The Nolan family really acted glad to have me back. They treat me as if we had been the best of friends always. It's fun to have friends who aren't just people you play chess with. Josie says they have a chess team at school and I should try out for it. Jason thinks I should try basketball, too, and he's going to take me to the gym and teach me how. You know the trouble I have thinking of things to say to people? I'm not that way around the Nolans, and it feels really good. If my stay here were a chess game, I would say this had been a successful "opening."

I *am* keeping track of what happens and writing it down for you. So far, some really mysterious stuff is going on between Josie Nolan and a girl named Tory Mitchell. I'm not going to send it on to you until I can figure out what's happening. (Remember, I only promised to report on winning moves!)

The puzzle clues start here:

It's cold and the whole town looks like VANILLA ICE CREAM.

Josie Nolan is neat looking. Her hair is kind of COCOA colored and her eyes are like soft CHOCOLATE. The Nolans have a Llaso Apso dog. Miss Pod is her name, and she is HONEY and CREAM colored. What a strange little monster she is! She'll kill for a BISCUIT.

Now, the test: Have you noticed special words in capital letters? These are distress signals from a starving son. Grandma cooks twice as much for me as she does for herself and brags about what a good eater I am, but when I finish, my stomach is still growling.

Don't say anything to grandma. She would be real upset.

Mrs. Nolan feeds me when I am over there but I don't want to be a freeloader on my friends. I get so desperate that I imagine the pigeons outside my windows stuffed with SAGE DRESSING and browned in GRAVY.

I dream of HOT DOGS chasing each other over fields of crunchy PEANUT BUTTER.

I'm not asking for a raise in allowance, but if you can throw in some extra grocery money, I promise to put it all in one place, my stomach.

I can't wait to get your first letter.

Love,

Greg

P.S. 1. Cross your fingers! I try out for the chess team this coming week.
P.S. 2. Happy Belgium!

Part Two

THE
MIDDLE
GAME

8

The First Day

I FELT FUNNY ABOUT going by to pick up Josie to walk to school.

"Don't be silly," Jason told me. "I bet you don't even know where the old junior high is. And anyway, after you get there, you have to find the office and all." He paused, tightening his mouth in an angry way. "You'll be doing Josie a favor. She hasn't walked to school by herself since Tory moved here except when her so-called friend was pretending to be sick to get her way about something. Maybe you can take her mind off things."

Jason overestimated me when it came to my getting Josie's mind off "things." I'm just no good at small talk, and Josie didn't have much to say. When we passed the apartment building on the corner, I saw her look up at the windows where Tory had lived. It was only a quick glance.

The shoveled-back drifts of Christmas snow were stained with dirt and oil from the street. It was the first school day of the New Year and, boy, did the year have a long way to go to earn "Happy" for a first name!

Josie was really a *big* help. She took me to the office and then waited until they finished processing my entering the school. The paper work went fast because Mom had sent on everything they needed. They had all my material ready, even to a class schedule.

I was due at English and Josie at Social Studies, but both classes were down the same long hall. We were almost to my classroom when a girl in a red sweater called from behind us. She caught up and grabbed Josie by the arm, talking a mile a minute.

"Josie," she said, all in a rush. "Tell me about Tory Mitchell! Have you seen her? Is she all right?"

Josie stiffened. "She was at my house the other morning," she replied. "She was okay then. Why shouldn't she be?" Then, remembering, she looked over at me. "Melanie Harding, this is Greg Farrell. Greg's from Washington, D. C. He's going to stay here for six months."

Melanie swept me with a swift glance and said, "Oh, hi!" Then she turned back to Josie. "How can you say that, Josie Nolan? Sometimes people get *hurt* when stuff like that goes on!"

"Stuff like what?" Josie challenged.

"Attempted kidnapping, domestic violence." Melanie paused, her expression confused. "But you live right down the street from her. You must have seen the whole thing. Everybody said there were police cars and everything. It was a really big deal."

"That's silly," Josie said, starting to walk on with her back very stiff. "Somebody called the police, maybe for noise, I don't know. Anyway, Tory and her mother didn't like it and decided to move away."

"Decided!" Melanie scoffed. "Boy, are we ever getting different stories? I heard that somebody tried to kidnap Tory, and her mother had to call the police. Then the landlord told them to move because the disturbances had made them undesirable."

The halls were crowded. A lot of kids slowed down as they passed us, obviously trying to hear what was going on.

"I don't know anything about any of that," Josie replied crossly. "And what's more, I don't want to know."

"But you must have seen that big car with the Texas license," Melanie said stubbornly, following us down the hall.

"Texas," I thought to myself. I hadn't noticed the license plates on the big limousine I had seen there that night.

"It probably belongs to Tory's grandparents," Josie said, walking faster. "Now come on, Melanie, leave me alone. We have to get to class."

"Let me tell you," Melanie said, running along after us. "Everybody says Tory's father and grandparents were trying to kidnap her. They might have gotten away with it if Tory's mother hadn't called the police in time."

"But they can't do that," Josie protested, turning finally to look at her. "The court gave Tory's custody to her mother."

"See?" Melanie said, triumphant. "That's

why Mrs. Mitchell could get the police to come help her when Mr. Mitchell and his parents tried to take Tory away."

The bell clanged loud enough to make me jump. All around us, kids began scurrying the way they do when they think they are going to be tardy. Josie didn't scurry. She just stood there. Her lips were tight together and she blinked really fast. I knew she was fighting back tears, so I looked the other way and waited. After a minute she remembered me.

"Oh, Greg," she said in a really sick voice. "Come on, let's go to class."

I imagine she was late to class. I know I was. After I handed my slip from the office to the teacher, I looked around for a seat. Tory Mitchell was in the center row about halfway back. Even after seeing how she'd acted at the Nolans' house, I still thought she looked prettier than anybody ought to. She looked right through me as if I were a pane of window glass.

That was a long day. Only one kid came up to speak to me. He stopped me in the hall, grinned up at me, and stuck out his hand. "Ben Hogan, here," he said. "Josie told me to look out for you. She said you were a crack chess player. I'm a wrestler, myself. Good luck. I hope that team beats Roosevelt all hollow."

I made a note to ask Josie what he meant. When I did, she explained that Roosevelt was the name of the other junior high, the school our chess team would play against. Roosevelt had driven our wrestling team right down into the mat, so Ben probably really meant what he said.

At the end of school, when I went to pick up Josie by her locker, I saw her talking to Tory Mitchell. I hung back down the hall until they were through.

Even as far away as I was, I could tell Josie was talking very fast, very intensely, while Tory stood like a little princess with her nose in the air.

Only when Tory turned to walk away did I hear anything of what she was saying. I understood how Jason felt. I wanted to grab that kid and slap her hard, maybe shake some manners into her.

Her voice had come clear and cold. "Listen, Josie Nolan," she said. "I want you to know that you do *not* understand what's going on in my life. You don't understand from up about me or anything. And just don't kid yourself that all that sugary stuff is going to make me come to your house ever again."

Then she looked at me that sneering way. "Maybe your freaky guy-friend will go home with you."

Josie turned so she was facing her locker. I knew she was trying to keep anyone from seeing her cry. I waited until she turned around again before I walked up to her.

"It's not out of my way to walk home by your place," I told her.

She nodded without meeting my eyes.

"Jason said I ought to come by after school," I added. This was awkward. I didn't want to force myself on her but I didn't want to leave her like that, all shaken up and crying. "This is my round-about way of asking if you mind my walking home with you," I said. "That is, if you don't mind walking around with a freak."

She looked up at me and her eyes snapped. "Don't pay any attention to *her*! I'd like to walk with you." Then she paused, frowning a little. "If you don't mind, let's stall until we can be sure that somebody has already picked Tory up."

Tory was gone when we got outside. I made

73

myself talk about my classes and asked Josie what Ben Hogan had meant about Roosevelt. I've never been very good at just making conversation. I was even worse that day than usual. After I would think of something to say or ask about, a little pause would come while Josie dragged her mind back to me and where she was. The minute she quit talking and a little silence fell, I could almost see her thoughts turn back to Tory and the mean way she had acted.

It was warm and neat in the Nolan kitchen. Jason had beaten us home. He picked up his things from the chair beside him and told me to dig into the tray of sandwiches in the middle of the table. He had a book about basketball strategies that he explained to me while we ate. When the sandwiches were gone, we ate pretzels dipped in hot mustard.

Lollie sat right across from me at the table. This was the first I had really seen of her. She was a cute little blonde kid with wispy hair and no front teeth on the top. It was easy to imagine her worrying about ogres and ghosts. She picked out only peanut butter and jelly sandwiches and then fed about half of them to Miss Pod. When Lollie was full, she wiped her mouth on the back of her hand and spread out her homework. She had a workbook with colored pictures in it. She kept putting her pencil in her mouth, which left little stripes on her upper lip like cat whiskers. She whispered to herself when she read the problems.

When Mrs. Nolan got home, I put my stuff together to leave. Josie had stayed upstairs all afternoon. She must have heard her mother return because she was coming through the downstairs hall when the phone rang. She answered it, listened a minute, then called to her mother. "Do you have a phone number for Tory's mother?" she asked.

Mrs. Nolan stopped dead still. With her apron strings still dangling, she took the phone from Josie with a nod. After listening a minute, she said, "I'm really very sorry," in a strange, withdrawn tone of voice. "I can't help you."

Either the caller didn't hear her or asked something else, because after a minute she said the same thing again: "I'm sorry, but I can't help you."

Josie watched her mother put the phone back. "That was Mr. Mitchell," she said. "Tory told me again today that she's not going to come stay with us the way we planned."

Mrs. Nolan went back to her work without

meeting Josie's eyes. "The invitation is still open," she said. "We'll see."

On the way home, I decided that if science could trap the kind of electric tension that had been winging around that kitchen, we could tear down a lot of big power plants.

9

Opening Round

GRANDMA WAS WASHING potatoes to put into the oven when I got home. "There you are," she said, just like Mom always did. Then she grinned at me. "When your mother and I talked about your coming, I wondered how much I would be walking the floor, worrying about where you were."

"Oops," I said. "Should I have called?"

She shook her head. "I was just thinking, now that I know you better, I won't worry."

"Woman," I told her sternly, "don't get too sure of yourself. I have an unexplored capacity for creative devilment."

"*Sure* you do!" she said, holding up a potato to study it critically. "Do you think you could eat two of these baked potatoes? They aren't very big."

It sounded greedy to suggest she go for four, so I just nodded.

She slid three potatoes into the oven and turned back to me. "Which reminds me. The library board is having a dinner meeting right after work Wednesday night." She made a face. "One of the members owns the worst steak house in town, so naturally we meet there. Tell me what you'd like for a solitary supper and I'll fix it ahead."

The world's most wonderful idea exploded in my mind. The words appeared in brilliant neon, flashing across my brain in giant capital letters. JUNK FOOD! JUNK FOOD! JUNK FOOD! Double cheeseburgers with bacon spun in my head (two for good measure), extra large fries, king-sized chocolate shake, and—later—an ice cream stop!

I was proud of the control I had over my voice.

"Why don't I just go by a fast food place?" I asked, very casually. "We're having the first chess match that afternoon, and I don't know how late it will run."

Her smile flooded me with guilt. "That's so thoughtful of you, Greg," she said. "But I hate to do that to your stomach."

"Cast iron," I assured her. "Consider it done." Then, not wanting to risk a change of plans, I looked around for something to change the subject.

Grandma always has a book nearby, even when she's cooking. The one by her plate on the table had a paper napkin stuck in it for a marker. I opened it up and read a few lines in the middle. "Is this good?" I asked her.

She grinned over her shoulder at me. "I don't know yet," she admitted.

I laughed. "You don't have much left to read. When are you going to decide?"

"When it washes back," she said, a little defensively. "Lots of times I don't really get the full sense of what I'm reading until I've finished. My mind stores up unanswered questions and scenes that didn't seem important. But after I read the ending, my mind flows back." She grinned. "Like something spilled on the kitchen floor. If the book was good and honest, everything

79

makes sense and fits in, and I'm satisfied."

What a lady! I studied her. Chess is like that, too. Your opponent makes moves you don't understand until the game is over. *Then* you understand, usually in defeat, what he had been working toward all that time. "Wash back," I said aloud. "That's great. That's really great."

All day I'd been puzzling over what Melanie had said about the excitement at Tory's house. I still didn't have any idea of what was going on. Maybe I just didn't know enough about the situation to be able to "wash back" and have it make sense. But Grandma lived in Pineville. She might know.

"Did you hear about the attempted kidnapping of Tory Mitchell?" I asked her.

She nodded the same brisk way Mom does. "If this town excels in one thing, it's gossip. You'd think the streets were lined with grapevines, the way news travels."

"You heard the story, then?" I asked her.

"*Everybody* heard the story," she said dryly. "Some of us several times. One of the joys of being a public servant."

"Tell me everything you know about it."

She frowned at me. "That's a funny thing to ask."

"I've got a lot of bits and pieces that don't fit together. I may not have a clean mind but it's very orderly."

She laughed. "Having you here is like having your mother back." She sat down across from me, her brow furrowed. "Now, let's see how it went."

"Start with the divorce," I suggested.

"Clear back there? It dragged on all summer, the way divorces do, and was final in October. Mrs. Mitchell got custody of the child, Victoria, with visiting and alternate holiday rights for the father."

"What does alternate holiday rights mean?" I asked. I had heard a lot about divorce without hearing that one.

"The child spends one holiday with one parent and the next with the other. And so on. I understand Victoria and her father went to Texas over Thanksgiving to visit his parents, who have a ranch down there. Then she had Christmas with her mother here."

"Why would the court set up a custody arrangement like that?" I asked.

She shrugged. "Probably so that each of her parents could enjoy every holiday with her, sooner or later."

I nodded. That made sense. But if Tory had been in Texas for Thanksgiving only the month before, it was strange that the grandparents were here at Christmas. But then, they did have a perfect right to visit their son, Tory's mysterious but marvelous father.

Grandma went on patiently. "The night of the supposed kidnapping attempt, the child had been left alone in that apartment. The father and grandparents claimed the mother was neglecting her by leaving her like that. That's why they came and tried to take her away."

Grandma's story was not helping very much. In fact, it raised as many questions as it answered. Tory shouldn't have been at the apartment at all. She was supposed to spend the evening with the Nolans. So how could Tory's father and grandparents have known she was home alone unless Tory herself had called and told them? I remembered Josie, standing at the phone and dialing over and over, and only getting a busy signal. As soon as Tory had finished insulting me, she must have marched straight home and called them.

"Mrs. Mitchell came back home before they got her away. When the mother couldn't handle the father and his parents, she called the police. That's all I know," Grandma said, rising and going back to the stove. She opened the oven door to check the potatoes. She must have put a meat loaf in just before I arrived, because that smell suddenly filled the kitchen. I went in by the fire and ate apples steadily until she called me to dinner.

The chess club didn't meet until after school on Wednesday. By then I had already figured out that my junior high in Pineville was different from my school at home, without being easier. My social studies teacher rumbled when he talked, which was sort of comfortable to listen to. My English teacher had a distracting habit of staring out the window while he lectured. If I could break myself of looking out to see what he saw, I would be able to deal with that class. My algebra teacher had a sense of humor. The vote was still out on my other teachers.

Josie and I had walked to and from school together each day. On Tuesday night Jason had taken me to the gym and we'd fooled around with the basketball. He was right. I wasn't half as awkward as I used to be. But I worked up such a sweat in half an hour that Jason laughed at me. "First we get you in shape!" he said. When I went back home with him for a snack, I'd been so hungry my stomach was echoing after running around that basketball court.

I knew I was in the right room for the chess club when I saw the woman sitting by the window, knitting. She had to be Mrs. Ryan from the music department. She looked up without stopping her needles or dropping a stitch. The sweater she was working on had a pattern of deep-sculptured diamonds and something that looked like kernels of popcorn, all made out of wool. She was a solidly built woman whose earrings looked like fishing spinners. "You must be Greg Farrell," she decided. "You have wonderful press."

I nodded and moved the rule book from the seat beside her and sat down. When you are as tall as I am, the closer you get to eye level with teachers, the less nervous they are.

"How do you think we ought to run the try-outs?" she asked.

Her question startled me. Then she went on. "We have six kids in the club, counting you."

"Six," I said. I don't know what I expected—maybe ten, or twenty like we had back home.

"Six," she repeated. "But we can only use three on the team. Jamie plays up and down, no one can predict him. Chad is a rank beginner."

"Rank and file?" I asked. At her confused look, I realized she *really* didn't know anything about chess. One of the first things you learn in chess is that the horizontal lines on a chessboard are called ranks and the vertical lines are called files. "Chess joke," I explained.

She smiled weakly and went on. "Melanie gets better all the time. Josie Nolan taught both Chad and Melanie to play."

"She also taught Tory Mitchell," I reminded her, because Josie had told me that.

"That's different," Miss Ryan said, wrapping her wool around the needles and laying them down. "I think the fairest way is for every player to play every other player. The ones with the three highest scores will have slots one, two, and three." Her smile was warm and satisfying. "And everybody will get a lot of good practice."

She was right, of course. I just crossed my fingers that Josie would be matched against one of the weaker players the first round. The last thing she needed was a failure of any kind right then.

The first round went fast. Josie played

against Chad, a broad-faced, friendly looking kid who puffed his cheeks out and blew a thin stream of air all the time he was thinking. Josie won but Chad almost blew her away in the process of losing.

I drew Jamie, who played a brilliant opening, then went all to pieces. I didn't watch Tory's game against Melanie but it didn't last long. Tory won.

Since it was early, we went for a second round. Two of the games were over right away. Jamie defeated Chad quickly. I tried to make the game with Melanie last a long time but I couldn't. After I defeated her, Tory and Josie had to play against each other.

It was a good thing Jason wasn't there. He might well have killed Tory. Any game that pits two people against each other becomes a contest in psychology as well as skill. Tory was playing it for all it was worth.

She never seemed to look at the board. The minute Josie moved a piece and lifted her hand, Tory reached down and moved a piece with the speed of lightning. She didn't say a word but she never took her eyes off Josie's face except for that split second when she was moving a piece. All the time she kept whistling softly between her teeth, as if she were bored with the whole thing.

Josie wasn't making her moves slowly, but she tried to speed up anyway. That kind of pushing gets you very uptight. Tory put Josie on the defensive from the first. Tory started whistling faster. Finally Josie was so rattled that she let both her king and queen fall under the control of the same knight. Tory spoke for the first time in a sneering tone.

"Check. Guard your queen."

By the rules of chess, Josie had to move the king away from the knight's control. With her queen gone, Tory finished her off.

Score at the end of two rounds:

Tory 2, Greg 2, Josie 1, Melanie 0, Chad 0, Jamie 1.

I had to check out some books and Josie waited for me. As we started out of the school to go home, we passed Tory, who was using the public phone just inside the front door. I figured she was calling for a ride home. When she saw us, she turned her back as we walked past.

It was dark and so cold that huge clouds of

spun-sugar light circled the street lamps. Any words you said smoked out of your mouth. I couldn't say anything to Josie that she didn't already know. She knew I was sorry. She knew Tory had played in an unsportsmanlike manner. She probably even knew that a good coach would have put a stop to that performance of Tory's at about the third move.

I stopped outside the front door of Josie's house. It was too late to go inside. Anyway, Jason had basketball practice on Wednesday and wouldn't be there. I would have given anything right then to be good with words. I managed to say the only thing that I could. "I'm sorry, Josie."

When she glanced up at me, the porch light turned her skin a funny golden color. She didn't look much like she had the first night I came. Her face was pinched and her eyes too big for the rest of her features. Her voice was as lifeless as her eyes.

"I'm not that upset about the game, Greg," she said. "Tory hates me, and I don't even know why."

I kicked snow all the way home. If my mom could have heard the words I was saying, she would have stopped my allowance for a good month. All my life I have wished I was that kind of kid who had a lot of good friends. Maybe I was lucky and didn't know it. If a friend could turn on you like that and make you as miserable as Josie was, who needed one?

And I wasn't in much better shape. I had come to Pineville, gotten to be friends with Jason and Josie, and then felt as miserable for Josie as I could have for myself. But Josie had asked the right question.

What would turn a friendship to hatred after all that time? It was as mysterious as it was painful.

10

Discoveries

I WAS HALFWAY TO Grandma's house before I re-membered she would be at her board meeting. I wished she was going to be home. I wanted somebody to talk to the way I used to talk to Mom, like we did the day she first told me about having to leave home for six months.

I slowed down, remembering.

I should have known that something big was coming up when Mom took me out in the car on a cold, rainy November day. She drove south out of Arlington and didn't say anything until we were away from the city traffic.

I learned early on that when Mom has something really important to talk to me about, she takes me out for a ride. I used to think she did it to avoid interruptions, like telephones or unexpected visitors. I've changed my mind. I think in her brisk, grown-up way she's as shy as I am, even with her own son. You see, when she is driving a car in traffic, she has to watch the road. She can keep her eyes straight ahead and talk about things to me that she couldn't possibly say face-to-face. With the windshield wipers swaying lazily back and forth, she dropped her little bomb.

"This is going to come as a blow, Greg, but it's absolutely necessary for me to spend six months working in Europe, starting the first of the year."

I could tell from her quick intake of breath how hard those words had been for her to say. I could also tell she wasn't through.

"Naturally I wish I could take you along with me. The honest truth is that I can't." Another quick breath. "The most sensible plan is for you to spend those months with your grandmother and go to school in Pineville until I get back."

She waited silently for me to reply. I really

wanted to respond with something, but it was important not to say the wrong thing. What I said had to be true. One thing Mom and I don't do is fool around with the truth. We only have each other and you have to have *someone* you can trust.

I've often wondered how it feels to have two parents instead of one. But things could be worse. I could have a mother I didn't get along with, or one who made important decisions all by herself and then expected me to live with them.

"Is this business in Europe something you want to do?" I asked.

She didn't look my way but I could hear the smile in her voice. "Let's say it's something I *have* to do to stay in line for the next promotion."

Mom's only got me and her work, and some day I will be off and gone. Then all she will have left is her work. Still, it didn't seem right that anyone was asking her to do something like this, even for some future promotion.

"Do those people know you are alone with only a twelve-year-old kid?" I asked.

This time the smile was broad enough to show on her face from the side. "Those people, as you call them, don't know or care about anything but the work I do. People show some polite concern about your life but the end result is the important thing. A lot of people really believe that any means will justify the right end."

I whistled softly. "My mother, the cynic."

That time she really laughed and mimicked my tone of voice. "My son, the kid who knows too many big words," she came back at me. This with a pat on the knee. "It's all right to understand it, just don't be guilty of it."

Thinking about Mom, I had slowed down. Remembering those words Mom said stopped me cold: "A lot of people really believe that any means will justify the right end."

Tory.

I stood staring at Pineville's frozen drifts, not seeing them. What was the matter with me? I'm a chess player. Why hadn't I put two and two together and gotten four with this business about Tory?

That's just what Tory was doing. She wanted to live with her father and she was using any means she could find to reach that end. She had already set up the situation of looking neglected by going home from Josie's. She had probably told her father that ugly story about Josie's "entertaining" a boy when she was supposed to be baby-sitting. What would she think up next? The thought scared me.

I came out of that trance conscious of two painful facts. My feet were blocks of ice and I *needed* to talk to somebody about Tory Mitchell.

I had forgotten about wanting to stuff myself with junk food. I wasn't even interested in eating at all. I only wanted to run my theory past someone I really respected. Jason. I pulled back my mitten and held my watch under the street lamp. He should be almost home from basketball. But if I went over there, Mrs. Nolan would ask me to dinner. I had to get him off alone for this talk.

Back to junk food! Still under the street lamp, I counted my money. I could invite Jason to eat with me if we both held the line at two cheeseburgers with trimmings and skipped the ice cream.

I didn't even stop to think whether a sixteen year old would want to be seen with a junior-high kid in public. It was vital that I catch him before his mother got dinner ready to serve.

I set off for the Nolan house running. Instead of staying on the cleared sidewalks, I cut through somebody's side yard and came out around the corner from the Nolan house.

A taxi was parked right beside that apartment building where Tory used to live, and the motor was running. Even though I ran way around it, I was still coughing from the fumes when I got to the Nolans' front porch and rang the bell.

Josie opened the door. "Hi," I said, suddenly self-conscious. "I need to ask Jason something."

She hesitated, "I'm not sure he's home yet. He had basketball practice."

"Jason?" Mrs. Nolan called from the kitchen. "He's just coming in through the garage."

Then Jason was there, and I was embarrassed again. "This is an invitation," I blurted out. "Grandma is eating at the worst steak house in town with the library board."

Mrs. Nolan chuckled. "Three guesses."

"Anyway," I went on, "I thought maybe you'd like to go have some cheeseburgers with me, Jason. My treat."

"Listen, you boys," Mrs. Nolan said. "I have a pot roast here that will stretch like elastic. Why don't you just eat with us, Greg?"

"Mom," Jason howled. "What are you saying? I get pot roast on pot roast here. The man is asking me out. I am accepting."

She chuckled. "It's your stomach lining."

"Cast iron," I told her.

"Sure, Greg." She grinned. "Have fun, you two."

With both of us walking fast side by side, we made our own cloud of frozen breath as we moved along. We had only taken a few steps when we heard Miss Pod start barking frantically inside the house.

"What's that all about?" I asked.

Jason shook his head. "She guards the world, that one. She's imagining something is wrong."

"Isn't she ever right?" I asked.

He glanced back at the house. "Sometimes. Mom will check it out."

Around the corner, the cab driver was still hunched down in the driver's seat of his taxi, trying to keep warm while he waited for his passenger. His exhaust fumes fouled the air for half a block.

"Keeping that cab waiting is costing somebody a bundle," Jason said. "Come this way. I know a shortcut."

11

The Tree House

I COULDN'T BELIEVE Jason had me running again so soon. By the time we reached the restaurant, I was both out of breath and starving. Worse than that, I couldn't think how to start talking about Tory to Jason. I needed somebody to help me figure out what was going on. But if I didn't manage it right, Jason would just lose his temper and start yelling. I decided to wait and see if the proper words wouldn't come to me on a full stomach.

I had forgotten how good a cheeseburger—make that two cheeseburgers—with bacon could be. Jason was full of basketball practice talk. I just ate and listened, relieved that he hadn't asked how the chess matches turned out. Some kids drifted in and out. They spoke to Jason and nodded to me. It was neat and great, but I still had to bring up the subject of Tory Mitchell.

Jason admitted it was his lunch money for the rest of the week but, between what he had on him and what I had left over, we could afford chocolate sundaes. We were at the counter and Jason was trying to talk the girl into extra whipped cream when the man in a trench coat and knitted cap came in.

He nodded at Jason and started toward the sandwich order desk. Before he got there, he turned. "Hey," he said. "Aren't you the Nolan boy that plays basketball?"

"Yes, sir," Jason said, straightening up a little.

"I just tried to drive down your street and couldn't get through," the man said. "What's going on with all the fire equipment?"

"Fire equipment?" Jason asked, looking at me. "Are you sure? We just came from there."

He shrugged. "You live in Grandpa Nolan's old house, don't you? The one with the porches? It looked like the fire was out back."

Jason was pushing his money toward the girl and she was pushing the sundaes toward him. "Forget it," he told her, leaving the coins all spread out. "Come on, Farrell, let's go."

We ran all the way back. Jason didn't miss a stride until we got to the corner down where Tory had lived. Then he sort of stumbled and said, "Oh, my God."

I guess we'd sat there feeding our faces longer than we thought. It was plain that we had missed the worst of it. The whole block was filled with emergency equipment. Streams of water still rose to the roof of the Nolan house and the houses next to it. The street was filled with people huddled together, some of them under blankets. A child was crying and, from somewhere, I heard Miss Pod's frantic bark, hoarser and deeper than usual.

There was still smoke, lots of it, and once in a while a pillar of scarlet flame shot up from around the back. That terrifying light illuminated the house like a bizarre fairy castle. The ice was everywhere. The roof was crusted with it, and glistening frozen pillars rose in strange places along the sides of the porches. Icicles as thick as a man's waist joined the roof to the ground.

"My God," Jason breathed again, as he started shouldering his way through the crowd toward his family.

Mr. Nolan held Lollie, her face buried in his neck. She was sobbing in a dull, rhythmic way. Mrs. Nolan, one arm around Josie, clutched the frantic dog without seeming to notice her. Like her husband, she simply stared, stunned even past crying.

At Jason's question, his father shook his head. "The fire must have started in the tree house," he said dully. "The one Dad built. The fire had a good start." He glanced at his wife and tried for a smile he didn't get. "That crazy little dog warned us, but by the time we quit trying to make her shut up and looked out there, things were out of hand."

"The tree house," Jason kept repeating over and over.

Pretty soon I was colder than I ever had been in my life. Mrs. Nolan draped a scarf over Lollie's face for fear of frostbite. When Mr. Nolan went to talk to the firemen, he came back looking worried. The family would only be allowed to go back into the house for necessary things. They had to spend the night somewhere else.

When I first asked them to come home with me to Grandma's house, they wouldn't hear of it. All of us kept getting colder. Finally I got as brisk and bossy as Mom herself.

"If it was Grandma and me, would you let us go to a motel?" I challenged Mrs. Nolan. I was freezing to death but unable to leave until they did.

Mr. Nolan looked at me for a long moment. "Tell you what, Greg. You and Jason take the girls to your grandmother's and settle them down. Mom and I will be along."

"And Miss Pod," Lollie sobbed.

"And Miss Pod," he promised.

Grandma does not have the largest house in Pineville, but it was big enough that night.

She has this blue bathrobe that laps over and ties on with a belt. I don't know what they call that material but it has fuzzy ridges with smooth places in between, sort of like some bedspreads. She was wearing that robe when we got there and, believe it or not, she made it look as brisk and businesslike as a sweater and skirt.

Jason and I built the biggest fire that hearth ever saw, and Grandma made cocoa for us kids.

When Mr. and Mrs. Nolan finally got there, she made coffee. It smelled wonderful, even though I can't stand the taste of the stuff. By that time Lollie and Miss Pod were both settled down, up in Mom's old room where I had been staying.

The rest of us ate tuna fish and egg salad sandwiches made with eggs that were still warm from being boiled. We saw some footage of the fire on the TV news. "Three Alarm Fire of Undetermined Origin." That was the first time I saw Mrs. Nolan even close to crying.

Finally everybody settled down, or seemed to. Josie went upstairs to sleep with Lollie and Miss Pod. Grandma moved a stack of books off the bed in the guest room and put the Nolans in there. Jason and I bunked down by the fire.

If Jason and I hadn't been friends before that night, we would have been afterward. For a long time we ate apples and watched the flames. After we both stretched out with pillows and blankets, Jason began to talk about Grandpa Nolan.

He started with how his grandfather had peeled apples so that the paring came off in a single long strip. After that he just rambled on with one story after another. I didn't really understand why he was talking like that until he mentioned the chestnut tree that had burned in the fire.

"Grandpa bought that lot to build his house on because of that tree," Jason told me. "When Dad got big enough to climb the tree, Grandpa designed the tree house and made it himself."

He stared in the fire for a long time without saying anything. "I never really felt Grandpa was dead as long as that tree was there, holding up the tree house he had made for Dad and Josie and me."

When he turned over and buried his head in his pillow, I tried not to hear anything but the sounds of the house settling for the night and the soft thud of the final ashes dropping to the hearth.

12

Advantages

EVEN THOUGH THE Nolan house didn't catch on fire, except for an open porch under the tree house, it was badly damaged, mostly from forced water and ice. Mrs. Nolan had to stay home from work the rest of that week for insurance people and decorators to make estimates.

Josie and I missed all that. When Mrs. Ryan realized we needed to have our chess team chosen by the weekend, she scheduled after-school matches for both Thursday and Friday.

The kids at school couldn't talk about anything but the fire. Josie shook her head at their questions, but her face looked hard and angry when someone added, "Boy, were you lucky that nothing much but that old tree house got burned!"

She didn't say anything about the chess matches, but she got a dogged look on her face that I sure understood. If I had to play chess in the same room with Tory Mitchell the rest of my life, I would give up the game.

Four of us were in the running at the start of the third round. Tory and I had two points each. Josie and Jamie were tied with one.

By the time the play ended, everything was turned around. Mrs. Ryan had said Jamie was unpredictable. What an understatement. He swept his forces across the board against Melanie like a Mongol horde. I still don't know where my head was during my game with Josie. She boxed me in so badly that I had to concede check.

Having Josie beat me was the best thing that could have happened. Losing a game you thought you would win is like being hit with a brick. It gets your attention. Since I had to play against Tory in the fourth round, I was glad Josie had waked me up.

You have to give Tory credit. She's good at chess. She thinks fast. She is aggressive enough to take control at her first turn. But she kept playing her pieces as fast as she could move them. I was lucky. She lost track for a minute and I won the game.

We would play the fifth and last round after school on Friday. Tory, Jamie, and I each had three points, with Josie and Melanie right behind us with two games apiece. Chad didn't get any points for being a graceful and constant loser but he sure deserved them.

When I dropped Josie off on the way home, I waved at Jason, who was coming in from basketball practice. Josie asked me in, but a strange car was parked in front of the Nolan house and, anyway, it was late.

Grandma's front porch smelled like garlic but, the minute I stepped inside, the tomato and basil chimed in. She was watching the evening news on TV.

"Spaghetti," I called to her. "Wonderful."

"Spaghetti wonderful yourself," she called back. "Plus an old-fashioned hello."

I laughed and went in to drop down on the divan beside her.

"You missed the report about the Nolan fire," she told me. "The investigation is still incomplete, but so far no evidence of arson has been found. They suggested the fire could be due to careless use of smoking materials."

I stared at her. "Nobody over there smokes."

She shrugged and grinned at me. "That may be arson squad lingo for 'I haven't the vaguest idea.' That sure is a nice family. I like it that you brought them home with you last night."

"I like it that you didn't mind," I told her.

She stared at me thoughtfully. "In all the excitement about the fire, I forgot that on the way home from the meeting I heard the little Mitchell girl was missing. Did they find her all right?"

I nodded. "It was a false alarm. Tory has been taking a cab to and from school since she moved out of the apartment house. She got the directions wrong for the cab driver last night. She made it home all right, but not until her mother was worried enough to call around."

Grandma shook her head. "It doesn't seem like Pineville when a kid has to take a cab home from school. But those new developments out there could confuse a homing pigeon."

When Jason rang the doorbell a little after eight, I was up in my room banging out an English theme. I heard the rumble of his voice talking to Grandma and went downstairs. I could tell he was mad from the way he was standing with his hands in his pockets.

"What's up?" I asked.

"Me, for one thing," he said. "Mom said to settle down or go run around the block." He grinned. "I chose your block. Actually," he said after a minute, "let's both run around the block. Game?"

He didn't run but started off walking fast. We hadn't gone a half block before he began talking, almost yelling at me. "Good advice, Farrell. I got real good advice for you. Don't grow up! Stop right where you are. Don't ever be a teenager. Boy, do they know about teenagers . . . just ask them. Teenagers drink, teenagers crash cars into other people, they smoke everything that will roll into a piece of paper. They practically set their own houses on fire."

"Hey, guy," I told him. "Slow down. What ticked you off like this?"

He turned and glared at me. "Guess what was waiting for me when I got home tonight? Some wise guy from the arson squad. I know where they got the word 'fuzz.' That was the fuzziest-talking man I ever listened to."

He deepened his voice to imitate the investigator. " 'We have established that you were not in your house when that fire started in the tree house. We have it on good authority that you and your friends have made a habit of smoking out there, one substance or another.' And on and on and on."

I stared at him. "But you're an athlete."

That broke the spell. He looked over at me and roared with laughter. "Look who doesn't read the papers! Athletes have been known to slip from the straight and narrow."

"Okay, okay," I admitted. "What was all this good authority he was quoting?"

"Dad called him on that. Dad even told him I had been out with a friend during the time the fire started, and offered to give him help in checking my movements. The guy laughed and said the statement of another kid wasn't going to carry any weight. Dad finally scared him off by dropping a few choice words like libel and defamation of character."

I looked at him. So another kid's word wasn't going to carry any weight? I resented that. I happened to be the other kid! The idea that hit me right then seemed so good and so logical that I was afraid of it. Jason was still sputtering and fuming when I interrupted him. "Jason," I said. "Do you have any money?"

He frowned, stepped under a street lamp, and emptied his pockets. "Three bucks. What do you need?"

"Ice cream," I told him. "Let's try an experiment."

The same girl was working behind the counter. Some guy bought two hamburgers with fries and coffee and counted his money out in change. When she finished ringing it up, she turned to us.

"Oh, hey," she said. "You're the guys who ordered the sundaes and then went off and left them!"

"Right," I told her. "We want two more of the same, and this time we'll eat them."

"Let me talk to my boss," she said. She disappeared into the back and returned in a minute with the manager.

"So that big fire was at your place?" he asked. "I couldn't figure out why you kids would buy that stuff, pay for it, and then rush out of here like that. Then the other guy who was in here told me the fire was right behind your house. I saw the pictures that night on TV. Things okay over there now?"

"Pretty much," Jason said.

"Donna thinks I should give you kids sundaes for half price since it wasn't your fault you couldn't eat them."

"That would be sporting," Jason said, grinning.

Neither of us said anything until we got our sundaes and were seated in a booth. "Is this your experiment?" Jason asked while we spooned our way through the whipped cream.

I was really tickled. I love it when things work like I want them to. "You know," I told him. "When Tory Mitchell called me a freak, I didn't like it much. But being a freak has its advantages, too. People remember freaks, even just big guys like us. We had been in this place for half an hour before that fire caught hold. Before that I had been at chess club and you'd been at basketball practice. If that guy from the arson squad decides to press his case, how many witnesses do you think we would have right here in this place?"

Jason grinned and caught a drip of chocolate at the side of his mouth with his tongue.

"Good thinking, Farrell. Should we go talk to the manager and the girl about it?"

I shook my head. "That would only make the guy from the arson squad think we set it up. Don't worry. That manager isn't going to forget any two kids he gave half-price sundaes to."

Jason looked at me and shook his head. "You have one really good head, Farrell."

"We chess players are big on strategy," I told him.

"I'm into slam-dunks myself," he said. "I only wish we had enough money to buy seconds."

Part Three

THE
END
GAME

13

Check

IT DIDN'T OCCUR TO me until we were into the fifth and last round that a tie was possible. I was mad at myself for not seeing it coming. Mrs. Ryan had finished the body of her sweater and was working on a sleeve with a ladder of diamonds running up it. When she called out the pairings for the Friday matches, I blew my breath out the way Chad always did.

My opponent was Chad. With no over-confidence intended, that win would put my score at four. Tory Mitchell was to play Jamie. The chances of Jamie's beating Tory were about one in five thousand. He had his brilliant moments but he was not in her league. Another win for Tory would give her four points. I was going to have to play against Tory Mitchell for the first position on the team. I had beaten Tory once. I wasn't sure I could beat her twice.

I watched her set up the board for her game against Jamie. She looked as if she were operating on another plane, off somewhere. Her cheeks blazed a bright pink and her eyes were brilliant and a little staring. Scary.

I was going to be on the chess team anyway, whether I placed first or second. I didn't care as much about winning first place as I did about having Tory lose it. I'd never faced a match like that. I'd *never* had strong personal feelings against an opponent before. It was an ugly feeling.

My loss of concentration was Chad's gain. I almost lost that game. While I was mulling the strategies I could use on Tory, Chad made steady moves toward a check. Luckily I realized what was happening in time to turn the game around and win. Tory defeated Jamie in a record number of moves. Melanie beat Josie, crying out "Check" in an unbelieving tone.

Josie didn't bat an eye. She had lost any

chance to be on the team by losing to Melanie, but she didn't seem to care. She shook Melanie's hand and began to put the chessmen away in that careful, methodical way that Grandpa Nolan had taught us.

Tory was looking at me from across the room, her mouth twisted in a little half smile. I stared back at Tory and thought about Grandpa Nolan. He had been a precise and careful player, with the endless patience for detail that makes a good strategist. But he never was a championship player. For the life of me, I couldn't think of anything he had ever said that would help me beat Tory Mitchell.

On the other hand, our chess coach back in Arlington had been a winner in college and then in regional championships.

I heard Mr. Micek's voice as if he were talking inside my head: "When you and your opponent are equally matched, you have to create an advantage beyond skill. The simplest way is to take him by surprise in every way you can think of. Play the game your opponent doesn't expect. Play in a style he doesn't expect. If you are usually a slow, careful player, play at the top safe speed you can handle. If you usually play a fast-paced game, slow it down until you use up every second on the time clock. If your opponent adjusts his rhythm to yours, switch styles instantly and throw him off balance again. If you are known as a quiet player, be talkative. If you usually have comments during the game, remain coldly silent."

Switch styles.

I can play fast chess; I just don't like to. I really love the game, love taking my time and enjoying every move. But if fast chess would disturb Tory Mitchell, she was going to get greased lightning. The other distraction would be harder for me to do. I'm not a talker, particularly during a game. But since Tory expected me to be quiet, she was going to get chatter if it killed me. I think talking all the time is hard work. You have to keep thinking of stuff to say. And it's never over. As soon as you've finished saying one thing, you have to start thinking of the next remark.

Naturally Tory got the white pawn and the privilege of starting the game. She sat very stiffly with that half smile still on her face. She didn't hesitate a moment but made her first move in a split second. As she did, I said, "Good luck, Tory!" as brightly as I could.

She was startled and tightened her lips in an annoyed way. I barely let her pawn touch the board before I played too. "Here's goes nothing," I said cheerfully.

Now she was really angry. I smiled back as genially as I could. "Your move," I told her.

She flushed a deep red and made another fast move. I followed with mine just as quickly. "Upward and onward," I said as I set the piece down.

Tory wasn't alone in her confusion. Everyone was watching in amazement. Mrs. Ryan rested her needles in her lap and looked over at us thoughtfully.

Tory was so mad that her hand trembled. "All right, Freak," she said furiously.

I almost couldn't believe my eyes. Clear back at the start of this story I explained what a gambit was. A gambit is a move in which a player gives up or sacrifices a game piece in order to get into a better winning position. A queen's gambit occurs when a player gives up the most powerful piece on the board—the queen.

Tory was trying a queen's gambit. She had let me take her queen even though she could have saved her. Earlier in the match, Tory had tried a queen's gambit with Josie and won the game with it. I couldn't believe she would be that daring in this final match.

If she intended to throw me off, she really did it. I desperately needed a minute to decide what to do. I stalled by looking up at her. "Aha!" I said. "The queen of the queen's gambit strikes again!"

Tory already had her hand above her piece when I spoke. She lifted her knight and stared at me in a strange, searching way. As I watched, her expression changed from surprise to fear. Little white lines came at the side of her mouth from how tight her lips were pressed together.

I couldn't believe she was going to move that knight. I know you're not interested in all the little details of the game but, if she moved *that* knight, she had no way of winning. I could checkmate her king in two moves.

Something had scared her. Whatever it was had startled her into a fatal mistake. Her hand trembled on the knight. Then she set it back down and picked up her queen's bishop.

I stared at her steadily, waiting for her to realize what she had done.

If you touch a piece during a game of chess you *have* to move it. The only exception occurs when you brush it by accident. Then you can say "I adjust" and move a different piece. Tory kept her eyes down as if she were waiting for my next move.

"I am sorry," I told her. "You didn't mention adjusting."

Mrs. Ryan was watching intently. "Something wrong?" she asked.

"Greg is calling me on some silly rule about touching a piece," Tory said scathingly.

Down went the needles, up came the rule book. Mrs. Ryan frowned through her glasses as she ran her finger along the index.

" 'Adjust,' " she said, and read the rule aloud. "You lifted your knight and then moved your bishop, didn't you, Tory?"

Tory ran her tongue along her lips and darted her eyes around the circle of watchers. "I guess I did," she said. "But that's just a silly technical rule, not a big thing."

Mrs. Ryan closed the book and laid it down. "The rules *are* the game," she said. "You must play the first piece you touched."

"But I can't," Tory protested.

"What do you mean, you can't?" Mrs. Ryan asked.

"He would have a checkmate."

Mrs. Ryan shook her head. "I don't have to look that up," she said. "You must either play the first piece you touched or cede the game to Greg Farrell."

Tory sat perfectly still. The only sound in the room was Chad letting out his breath in a slow, tense whistle.

Then Tory leaped to her feet. She caught the edge of the chessboard with her knee and sent the pieces clattering across the wooden floor. Somebody gasped, and Mrs. Ryan spoke sternly.

"All right, Victoria," she said coldly. "We accept that you cede the game. Now, pick up the men and put them in the box."

"Pick them up yourself," Tory shouted. "Better yet! Let Freak Farrell and his sappy girl-friend do it." She stamped across the room and slammed the door behind her.

Mrs. Ryan looked after her with a little frown. "I suppose we could go after her and make her come back." Then she shrugged. "That would only add a scene to a scene. Maybe one of you could be a good sport and pick up the chessmen."

I looked after Tory in a kind of daze. I felt as if something important had happened that I didn't understand. Why had Tory looked so scared? What had upset her so much that she made that stupid move?

When I turned around, Chad was already fishing chess pieces out from under the desks and chairs.

I made a mental note that when this tournament was over, I was going to coach that kid. He was too nice a guy to keep on finishing last.

14

The Queen's Gambit

JASON CALLED LATE that Friday night after Tory's tantrum. His voice sounded awfully serious over the phone.

"You've got to come over here tomorrow," he said. "Come early and plan to hang around."

"What's up?"

"Me," he said flatly. "I need you. Mrs. Mitchell is escaping to Minneapolis and Terrible Tory is moving in with us, lock, stock, and designer jeans. Mom is clearly out of her mind to let her come. Josie is giving an Academy Award-winning imitation of the walking dead, and I'm not to be trusted without a keeper. I could kill Tory Mitchell and be put away for life. Only your calm sanity can prevent that dread occurrence."

"But Tory hates me," I reminded him.

"What better recommendation could a guy have?"

Grandma dropped me off at the Nolans the next morning on her way to the library. Neither of the girls had even come down yet. Jason and I were eating pancakes in the kitchen when Miss Pod came barking down the stairs like a man-eating mop. Jason groaned as his mother went to the door.

I hadn't met Mrs. Mitchell but I was glad Mrs. Nolan didn't try to do introductions. Obviously Miss Pod knew her, because she quieted down to a lot of wagging when she saw who it was. Mrs. Mitchell, with a harried look, brought Tory, with her set of matched luggage, into the front hall. I heard her thanking Mrs. Nolan for keeping Tory for her. She added a worried, "You have my number in Minneapolis if you need to call."

I consider myself a fair judge of mothers. I would have put Mrs. Mitchell at about three straws short of the breaking point. And who would blame her? Tory stood there, stiff and unsmiling. She didn't even move when her mother leaned to kiss her on the cheek. "Aren't you going to tell me good-bye?" her mother asked.

"Good-bye," Tory said, just like that.

Beside me at the kitchen table, Jason was growling under his breath. Mrs. Nolan walked out to the cab with Tory's mother. When she got back, she looked at Tory doubtfully. "Wouldn't you like to take your things upstairs and put them away?"

"No, thank you," Tory said, still standing in the hall.

Mrs. Nolan hesitated. "Well, there's space in the closet and empty drawers when you are ready."

"Thank you," Tory said without moving.

If it hadn't been so awful it would have been funny. Tory just stood there in the front hall beside her luggage. Josie and Lollie were off upstairs somewhere. Miss Pod cocked her head and stared at Tory a moment, then settled herself on the floor beside the luggage.

Tory hadn't stood there very long before Lollie came bouncing down the stairs stiff legged, the way she sometimes did. She stopped on the bottom step and stared at Tory. "What are you waiting for?" she asked.

Tory pursed her mouth and looked away without answering. Lollie shrugged and hopped into the kitchen on one leg. She sat down in the chair beside Jason.

"What's she waiting for?" she asked him.

Jason shook his head. "Beats me," he said. "Don't worry, she probably won't need dusting until about Wednesday."

Lollie giggled behind her hand, because dusting was her part of the housecleaning work. She looked at Tory a few minutes curiously, then took a tangerine from the fruit bowl and began to peel it.

When Tory still hadn't moved after about an hour, I began to ask myself Lollie's question. What was she waiting for? The whole house felt like waiting. Mrs. Nolan came in and out of the kitchen on one errand after another. Her face looked a little more strained every time she walked through.

Jason went upstairs and came back with a board game. By the time we had played it twice, it was almost noon. Apparently Tory finally got tired of standing. She sat down on her suitcase and propped her chin in her hands. Miss Pod had fallen asleep in the hall beside her. When Tory moved, Miss Pod woke up, blinked at her, then settled back to sleep.

Waiting.

When Miss Pod leaped up and began to bark again, we all realized someone was coming. Tory was on her feet before Mrs. Nolan had a chance to cross the hall. The minute Mrs. Nolan opened the door, Tory shot past her and grabbed the tall, fair-haired man on the porch around the waist.

"Daddy, Daddy," she squealed. "You came. You came."

He cupped his hand around her head. "You knew I would," he told her. Then, turning to Mrs. Nolan, he said, "I have come for my daughter."

"Oh, but, Mr. Mitchell," she said, "you can't . . ."

"I can," he said firmly. Only then did another man appear in the doorway. "Mrs. Nolan, James Wade, my attorney."

As Mrs. Nolan stared at the second man and

then back at Tory's father, Jason rose quietly. He scooped up the frantically barking dog and went to stand beside his mother. "What is this?" she asked. "Why is your attorney here?"

With the corner of my eye, I saw Josie at the top of the stairs, silently watching. Lollie stared wide eyed from her chair in the kitchen. Tory, both arms tight around her father, beamed triumph at us with shining eyes.

The attorney was plainly not as comfortable with this as Tory was. He cleared his throat a couple of times as he opened his briefcase. "My client, Mr. Mitchell," he began, unfolding a paper, "has obtained a court order authorizing him to remove his child from your temporary care."

"But her mother . . ." Mrs. Nolan began.

Mr. Mitchell's smile was as cold as the draft from the open door. "We know about Mrs. Mitchell's arrangements to leave the child here. Upon my complaint, Judge Harkness issued the order that she be released to my custody."

"Complaint?" Mrs. Nolan asked, looking from one of them to the other. "On what grounds?"

"Mrs. Nolan, I have a natural father's concern about Victoria's environment. The judge agreed that Mrs. Mitchell's arrangements were not suitable."

Mrs. Nolan, usually at no loss for words, could only seem to echo what she heard. "Not suitable?" she repeated. "In what way, not suitable?"

The attorney's tone was soothing. "Surely you don't want the details aired in front of these children."

"Yes, she does," Jason said, glaring at Tory. "We all do."   .

At the attorney's startled glance, Mrs. Nolan nodded her agreement. He rattled the paper.

The charges had even been numbered. The Nolan family had a long record of consistent child neglect. They had been known to absent themselves from the house, leaving their pre-teen girl and a male friend alone in the house without a chaperone. The son of the family had been a consistent and long-term user of illegal substances, a habit which had recently threatened the family home with destruction by fire when he and his friends smoked in the family tree house.

"Need I go on?" the attorney asked. Mrs. Nolan's face had gone dead white as she laid her hand on Jason's arm.

"Libelous," she said. "Those charges are libelous. They simply aren't true. Where did you get all this?"

Astonishingly, Jason stood silent, as stunned as his mother. I felt the anger that he usually fought so unsuccessfully rising in me.

I looked past them at Tory Mitchell's face. The moment our eyes met, her expression changed. The stiffness of fear widened her eyes as it had in the chess game when I'd called her "The queen of the queen's gambit." I had only said that to buy myself time in the heat of the game. Yet the words had terrified her enough that she couldn't meet my eyes even now.

Queen's gambit.

It was so stunningly clear, so overwhelmingly awful, that I almost couldn't deal with it. I got to my feet so awkwardly that my chair fell behind me with a clatter.

"There's no mystery about where all that libelous stuff came from," I said, not even recognizing my own voice. I'm not a shouter usually, but I couldn't have spoken quietly right then for my life. "Ask her. Ask Tory, the queen of the gambit over there." As I spoke, Tory tightened her arms around her father, clinging to him.

"Don't listen to him, Daddy," she wailed.

"Let's go. Let's go right now. I've been waiting all this time."

I had to raise my voice to drown her out. "Great chess player, your daughter," I told Mr. Mitchell. "She made one great move after another. Tory was here with Josie the night she called to tell you her mother had left her alone. I know, because I came over to see the Nolan family. Tory waited until Josie went upstairs to tend to her little sister and then took off. I saw the police having to force her to get into her mother's station wagon. Tory was supposed to be *here* and she was, until she saw a chance to set her friend up."

Tory was wailing, begging her father to take her away, but I kept on talking. He stared at me, dumbfounded.

"As to the fire," I went on, "did anybody ever check into where *Tory* was all the time she was missing? Did she give the cab driver the wrong address as she said, or did she come over here and set that fire, with her taxi waiting around the corner? I saw the cab. Jason and I both saw it when we left to go out and eat. And we have about twenty witnesses who can tell you where *we* were when that fire was set. Who does

Tory have to back up *her* story of wandering around in a cab all that time? There can't be more than a couple of cab companies in this town. It should be easy enough to find the guy who brought her here."

Tory burst into tears and was sobbing against her father. He patted her shoulder nervously.

"I don't even know who you are," he said to me, his voice rising. "What business do you have in all this? What are you leading up to?"

"That's a high-risk kid you've got there," I told him, getting madder the longer I talked. "Trust a chess player to try a gambit like that. She told Josie from the first she would end up getting to live with you. Then she arranged it by setting up the only friends she ever had in this town. What a chess player, I mean. She outmaneuvered all of you, didn't she, even the judge who issued that paper? Boy, I hope you enjoy her. Just don't trust her as far as you can throw her."

Tory was crying wildly now, with her head pressed into her father's coat.

"Tory," her father said, trying to pull her face free so he could see her. "You talked to the judge. You couldn't have lied to him." She only clung to him, weeping.

Jason came to life. With Miss Pod still hooked under one arm, he silently reached down, picked up Tory's luggage, and carried it past her father through the open door.

The attorney looked from his client to Mrs. Nolan with a confused expression.

"You have your piece of paper," she told him. "Take the child."

I hadn't heard Josie come down the stairs. Suddenly she was just there, pale and tear stained but stiff backed.

"Good-bye, Tory," she said in the most final tone I have ever heard.

Tory's sob caught in her throat. She turned around and looked at Josie and then at me, a stunned expression on her face. Then her father was pulling her along.

Fury followed her shock. "Freak," she screamed. "Freak Farrell. That's all you are, a freak!" I could still hear the rhythm of her words after Jason pushed the heavy front door shut.

Lollie had begun to cry. Mrs. Nolan went to her automatically, leaving the rest of us standing in the sudden quiet of the hall. Josie turned and walked upstairs without looking back. She reached the fourth step before Miss Pod caught up with her and raced to the top to wait for her.

Jason was staring at me. "How did you know all that? How did you figure it out?"

I wanted to tell him "wash back" but knew he wouldn't understand. But that's what it had been. While the attorney was reading that paper, my mind had washed back over everything that had happened since the first time I came to the Nolan house. Mysterious things that seemed to have no connection fitted together, if you thought about them in terms of a gambit. Tory had used the classical strategy, sacrificing her best friend and her family to get her own way. No wonder she had been scared when I'd called her the queen of the gambit. But she had won after all, at what a price!

I only shrugged at Jason and grinned. "We chess players are big on strategy," I reminded him. "Big but slow."

Jason made coffee for his mother. She didn't even protest. She just sat by the table, with one arm around Lollie, staring at nothing. The coffee smelled fine but I could tell from her face when she tasted it that it wasn't very good.

"What about Tory's mother?" Jason asked.

"I'll have to call and tell her, after her plane lands and she reaches her hotel," Mrs. Nolan said.

"Do you *really* think she'll be surprised?" I asked.

Mrs. Nolan looked at me and smiled crookedly. "You're right, Greg. She might even be relieved to have a long, losing battle over." Then she set the coffee cup down and really smiled at me.

"Remind me to tell your mother what a good kid she's got," she told me. "Even if you are twelve years old going on a hundred."

"Never underestimate a freak, Mom," Jason told her.

Her shocked look left when she saw me grinning. She reached over and touched my hand, the way Mom always did when the words didn't come handy.

15

Queening the Pawn

THAT FIRST NIGHT I went to the Nolans, Josie and I had talked about all sorts of things, including birthdays. I'd teased her about being a kid. My birthday had come clear back in September, while she wouldn't turn twelve until January.

She had shrugged. "Never mind. August is a terribly dull month to have a birthday. You probably have the same old sunshine every time."

I admitted I probably did.

"Not me," she said. "It always snows on my birthday." Then she corrected herself. "Now, actually, Greg, that's not really accurate. Sometimes we get freezing rain or sleet. But I am the pampered darling of the sky. Other people's birthdays come and go with mixed weather reports. Not mine. As sure as my birthday dawns, the sky wraps up something cold and wet in a big howling wind and dumps it right on my life. 'Happy Birthday, Josie Nolan,' it shouts. 'Have a nice pneumonia!' "

When I laughed, she pretended to be indignant. "Just wait and see," she warned me. "It's coming up right away. We'll have some kind of nasty weather. You'd think a girl turning twelve would get a break. Sunshine, maybe, and streets you could get through without a dog sled? Wait and see!"

With all that had happened, I forgot about Josie's birthday until Mrs. Nolan called and invited me to join the family for dinner that next Monday night. "Not a party," she said. "Just Josie's special day, and we *all* want you here."

My room in Grandma's house is the same one that Mom had when she was little. Mom is tall for a woman, and I've wondered if she hit her head on the slant of the ceiling the way I do when I forget. But I really love that room. Even with the slanted ceiling, there are windows cut in all the walls. You feel very close to the sky up there.

On Josie's birthday, I knew without opening the curtains that the sky had sent her snow. The silence in the room told me so. Living in Illinois makes you an expert on winter weather. Sleet chimes against downspouts, and rain drums on the roof. Snow belongs to silence.

I lay listening to the silence and thought about my last birthday. My science teacher back in Virginia, Mr. Evans, was a very mellow man in class but a demon with tests. He talked science all the time. On the day I turned twelve, someone told him it was my birthday. He wished me good luck and added that in some cultures a twelve year old is considered a grown-up.

I don't think it makes any difference what your culture thinks, being grown up is something you decide inside yourself. I don't know what it's going to take to make me feel like a genuine card-carrying grown-up but I sure felt a lot closer to it that morning of Josie's birthday than I had when I came to Pineville.

When I came, all I really worried about was surviving that six months and getting back to my "real" life.

That seemed like a long time ago. My own survival, whatever that meant, seemed pretty unimportant compared to getting Josie back to being her old self. For really great people like the Nolans to be sacrificed to Tory Mitchell's selfish ends was bad enough. For Tory to get away with it and leave Josie quiet and downcast the way she had been was mega-wrong.

A lot I could do about it! I threw off the comforter and raced for the shower to get it off my mind.

Grandma was singing to herself when I got to the kitchen. Like Mom, she sings off key and hums where she has forgotten the words.

"I guess I'll be eating alone tonight," she said. "Wish Josie a happy birthday for me."

"I might even bring you a piece of cake," I teased. Then I remembered. "Hey, I never did decide on anything to give Josie for her birthday." When Grandma didn't answer, I looked up to see her laughing quietly to herself.

"You're beautiful when you panic," she told me. "Don't worry about it. I had something sent over."

"What is it?" I asked.

"Ha!" she said. "You think I'm going to tell you? No way. You fooled around until you almost blew it. You can just worry until she opens it tonight."

"What kind of a grandma are you?" I asked, really more amused than worried.

"The best kind," she said. "Tough! Just try not to look surprised and give us both away."

Boy, sometimes that woman is so much like Mom that I can hardly deal with her.

But I wasn't looking forward to that birthday dinner. As much as I like birthday cake, which generally arrives in a matched set with ice cream, I couldn't see how anybody could feel very happy after what Tory had put them through. Probably Lollie and Miss Pod would be the only ones there who wouldn't be hurting inside for Josie.

And there was still the chess business to get through. With Tory gone, somebody had to move up and take that third-place slot. Josie had already told me she wasn't going to do it.

"I just don't want to," she said. "That's all. I just don't want to play on that team. I may not even play the game again."

Somebody better with words might have argued with her. I didn't. I didn't even tell her how much more fun it would be for me if she were on the team. Sometimes I really envy people who always have the right thing ready to say.

After school that Monday, Mrs. Ryan was waiting by the window as usual. The unusual thing was that she hadn't even taken her knitting out of her bag. She was just sitting there watching the snow fall and waiting for us. When Chad went to the shelf for the chess sets, she shook her head.

"With this snow still coming down, I don't think we should play today." Jamie groaned and Melanie stuck her lower lip out as Mrs. Ryan went on. "I didn't cancel this meeting because we have some business to attend to."

Everyone was looking at her except Josie. "I am sure you have all heard that Tory Mitchell is leaving to go live with her grandparents in Texas."

At that Josie looked up, first at Mrs. Ryan and then at me, with an expression of absolute horror. I remembered what Tory had said that first night at Josie's house when I told her I was staying with my grandmother: "I wouldn't stay with my grandparents if they forced me to. I hate them. I'd run away and they could just look for me till the end of time." She had added that her dad was wonderful but his folks were the pits. "They live on a big ranch in Texas with horses and all the money in the world and snap at me every time I open my mouth." If Tory had spilled all that on me the first time we met, she must have gone on and on about her Texas grandparents to Josie.

Was it possible that Tory had fought the big fight but won and lost at the same time?

"We need to decide who will play third on the team," Mrs. Ryan went on. "As you know, Melanie and Josie are tied for the next place. Before anyone says anything, I'd like to suggest we give that third place slot to Melanie Harding."

All the kids stirred in their seats except Josie, who was frowning down at her hands, avoiding their eyes.

"You see," Mrs. Ryan went on, "I'm not any kind of a coach at all, but I do know how coaches act. I scouted around like a regular coach." She grinned as she admitted that. "I found out the teams that have chess coaches have a real advantage. The coaches travel with the teams wherever they go and are a big help to the players during the matches. I'll go everywhere but I can't offer anyone any help. Nobody on our staff can do that. The best chess teacher around is Josie Nolan. I'd like to propose that Josie be our coach. With her help, everybody's game would improve. And she could also fill any slot if someone were sick or unable to play."

Josie raised her eyes to stare at Mrs. Ryan. She had the strangest look on her face, a slow-dawning, happy look that hadn't been there for weeks.

"Would you consider doing that for us, Josie?" Mrs. Ryan asked. "Everyone on this team, including Tory, was taught by either you or your grandfather. Clearly you Nolans have a gift. A gift we need."

Jamie leaned forward to thump Josie on the shoulder. "Hey, coach," he said. "What a deal!"

Melanie was urging Josie with a whispered, "Do it! Do it!"

Josie never did answer in so many words. She only looked around at all of us and smiled that tight way you do when you don't want to give away how tickled you are. Then she nodded "Yes" to Mrs. Ryan.

"You could start with the worst player and

work up," Chad said, grinning over at her. "That way I'd get you to help me first."

Josie was a different kind of quiet going home. When we stopped on the porch to kick the snow off our boots, she looked at me in a funny way.

"Do me one favor, will you, Greg? Tell Dad what happened about the chess team."

"You sure you don't want to?" I asked her.

She nodded. "I couldn't," she said. "I don't know why, I just couldn't."

Nobody had told me that barbecued ribs were Josie's favorite meal. Apparently Miss Pod liked them, too, because instead of just planting herself by my chair to pump the air, she whined in the most pitiful way.

"A word of warning," Jason told me as I weakened and started to cut off a bite of rib without any fat for her. "Anyone who feeds that dog ribs has to wash the red sauce out of her beard."

I remembered those stiletto teeth of hers. That was that.

The baked potatoes were huge and Mrs. Nolan had the best salad I have eaten since I came to Illinois. I kept thinking I should tell Mr. Nolan about the chess team and not getting a chance to. Jason and I helped clear the table while Josie's dad brought a stack of presents in from the other room.

"Mine first!" Lollie squealed, bouncing up and down in her chair. In among the wrapped packages was one in florist's paper. I groaned to myself. Boy, if Grandma had done something sentimental, I would go through that floor.

You could tell Lollie had picked out her own present for Josie. It was a funny little plastic tree with no leaves on its branches. "It's for earrings," Lollie announced before the paper was all the way off. Josie made a big fuss about it and nobody mentioned that she didn't even wear earrings.

Her folks gave her the casette recorder she had asked for and a sweater in a great shade of blue. Jason gave her a hooded sweat shirt with his high-school insignia on it.

The pot of green shoots from the flower shop was from me. Thank goodness it had a green printed tag hooked to the ribbon. "Oxalis," Josie read. "Follow directions on reverse and this pot of shamrock will be blooming on St. Patrick's Day." She turned to me, looking astonished. "Shamrock! Greg, what a wonderful present. How did you ever think of it?"

"Just luck," I told her. "I have an Irish grand-mother."

Mrs. Nolan was getting matches to light the candles when I finally got my courage up. I don't think I had ever spoken directly to Josie's dad except when he asked me something. My voice cracked a little as I began. "Mr. Nolan," I said. When he glanced over at me, I thought for sure I wasn't going to get the words out past my Adam's apple.

"Yes, Greg?" he said, looking at me so intently that I got even more tongue-tied.

"A neat thing happened at our chess meeting today," I began, really fast. "Josie was appointed as the coach of the whole club."

He looked at me soberly a minute. "How did that come about?" he asked.

"Well," I began. Then it struck me again how great it was and I forgot to be self-conscious. "Did you realize that every one of us was taught to play chess by either Josie or Grandpa Nolan? Mrs. Ryan called it a gift. Anybody can play chess she said, but teaching it is a real gift."

He nodded thoughtfully without saying anything. I knew Josie was watching silently and held my breath. I was even beginning to get mad and resentful that Mr. Nolan was taking this so calmly. Didn't Josie's own father know how important this was?

When Mr. Nolan got up and left the room, we all just stared after him. Josie ducked her head a little and I was afraid for her that she was going to cry.

Then he was back. I heard Josie gasp, just a quick intake of breath as he set the walnut box that held Grandpa Nolan's chessmen in front of her. Then he leaned to kiss her cheek.

"Dad told me I should give you these when the right time came. Congratulations, Josie, and Happy Birthday."

Josie didn't say anything. She just opened the lid and stared at the chessmen a few moments before lifting out one of the pawns and holding it tightly in her hand. "Oh," she said then. Just the single word, repeated over and over. "Oh."

"Hey," her father said. "We better get those candles lit or you and your friend Greg won't have time for a game tonight. Tomorrow is a school day, Coach."

Josie moved in a dreamy way as if time had transformed her. After she replaced the pawn carefully, she smiled over at me, a slow warm smile that changed her face back to the old genial happy kid she had been.

"How about it, friend?" she asked me. "Are you up to the challenge?"

I remembered the first night when she had talked to me about her friend Tory. As rude as Tory was and as badly as she had been treating her, Josie had been defensive of her, making excuses, trying to make me appreciate what a great girl her friend was. Friend *wasn't* a word Josie used lightly. I didn't take it lightly when I grinned back and said, "You're on," while her mother lit twelve candles, one by one.

Talk about good breaks. I still had the remainder of my six months to spend in Pineville. At that moment I knew these would be the best six months of my life so far. I would play my heart out for this chess coach. Jason was going to make a basketball player out of me whether I wanted to be one or not, and I did. But best of all, as long as I was around, Josie would have a friend she could trust, I would see to that. And enjoy every minute of it.

Like everybody else in my family, I sing off key. All the Nolans did too, but nobody seemed to mind. We had such a good time that I almost felt sorry for Tory, who had blown all this and ended up in Texas where she didn't want to be.

Almost, but not quite. A gambit is a high-risk play you shouldn't try unless you're willing to live with the way the game turns out.

Notes on Chess
by Greg (Freak) Farrell

Since not everyone who reads this story is going to be a chess player, I thought it might be helpful to list some of the terms used in the game.

THE BOARD

Chess is played on a large square that is divided into sixty-four smaller squares. These small squares are alternately dark and light. The board is placed between the two players so that each one has a light square in the corner at his right. When you draw a chessboard on paper, the bottom edge is called the

"White" side and the top edge is called the "Black" side.

THE WHITE SIDE

Rank and File. The lines of squares on a chessboard are called ranks and files.

Files are the lines that run from the white side to the black. A file is named for the chess piece that stands on it at the beginning of a game. On the diagram, the names of White's files are written in.

Ranks are the lines that run parallel to the White and Black sides. Ranks are numbered from one to eight, away from the player. On the diagram you will see Black's numbers on the left and White's numbers on the right.

Moves are described by using the file name and rank number. For example, on the board shown, the ranks are numbered and the pawn move shown is called: Pawn to Queen 4.

1							8
2							7
3							6
4							5
5			♟				4
6							3
7							2
8							1

THE NAMES OF FILES

QUEEN'S ROOK FILE   QUEEN'S KNIGHT FILE   QUEEN'S BISHOP FILE   QUEEN'S FILE   KING'S FILE   KING'S BISHOP FILE   KING'S KNIGHT FILE   KING'S ROOK FILE

THE CHESS PIECES

Each player has sixteen pieces, all of the same color. These pieces are: one king, one queen, two bishops, two knights, two rooks or castles, and eight pawns. The pieces are set on the small squares of the board, with all the pieces, including the king and queen, facing a similar piece across the board.

Grandpa Nolan told me if it is easy to remember the pieces if you think of the game as a little war between two kingdoms. The king and queen begin the game in the safest possible place, with all their powers grouped around them. On each side of them are the bishops, who represent the power of the church. Next come the knights, the cavalry, mounted horsemen who can range around and protect their majesties. The rooks represent the castle walls that protect the kingdom from invasion. The pawns are the foot soldiers and form the kingdom's standing army.

The pieces, along with their powers, are described as follows.

The Kings (both black and white) are always the tallest pieces. A king can only move one square at a time. He can move on the rank (sidewise), on the file (frontward or backward), and on the diagonal. The king cannot move onto a square that is under attack by a piece from the other side. Two kings can never stand on adjacent squares.

The symbol for the king is his crown, which is shown like this:

The Queens are the second-tallest pieces. A queen can move in all directions and go as far as she wants, unless another piece blocks her way. Since she can move both in a straight line and on the diagonal, she has the powers of both a bishop and a castle. On a chess diagram, you can recognize a queen by the points on her crown, as shown:

The Rooks (or Castles) are round towers with castellated tops. A rook can move straight in any direction along an unobstructed rank or file—forward, backward, or sideways. Rooks can never travel on the diagonal. Rooks are shown as follows:

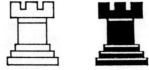

The Bishops are shaped like a clerical hat, usually with a cleft on one side. A bishop can move only on the diagonal and can move as far as he wants unless blocked. The bishop always stays on the color on which he began. Because of that, each player starts the game with one bishop on a light square and one on a dark.

The Knights are drawn to represent the heads of horses. The knight has the most interesting move. He doesn't travel on the rank or file, the way the other pieces do. He moves from point to point, so he can jump over a piece in his way. He can move one square forward and one square on the diagonal in a single play. A knight always ends his move on the opposite color from where he began it. For example, if he starts on white, he ends on black, and vice versa.

The Pawns are the shortest pieces, and they are usually the least powerful. The first time a pawn moves in a game, he can move either one or two squares straight forward on his file. After this first move, he can only progress one square at a time and always away from his owner's side of the board. (Soldiers cannot retreat.)

All chess pieces can capture the opponent's pieces. Except for the pawn, chess pieces *capture* by moving, each in its required manner, onto the square where its enemy is sitting. The captured piece is then removed from the board and replaced by the one that captured it.

Pawns capture differently. A pawn can't attack a piece standing in his way. This makes it hard to move pawns because you can block one just by setting something in front of him. However, a pawn can capture any piece that is one square ahead of him on the diagonal. When the game is in progress, a pawn out in the middle of the board has only two squares he can attack. If he is at the side (in either of the rook files), he has only one square he controls.

The pawn has one other small power. This is called *en passant,* which means "in passing." If a pawn has moved two squares in his first move and his opponent now moves two squares on either side of him, the first pawn out may capture the opposing pawn by moving into the square the other pawn skipped. He can only capture *en passant* as soon as the other pawn moves. If he doesn't do it then, he loses the chance forever.

This is the way pawns appear in diagrams:

Playing the Game

Before the game begins, one of the players conceals a black pawn in one hand and a white pawn in the other. He offers the back of his hands to his opponent, who chooses one by tapping the back of one of the hands. If the pawn inside the chosen hand is black, the player will use that color and the other person will start the game. White always gets the first move.

While it is said that the purpose of the game is

to capture the opponent's king, no king is ever really captured. When you bring a king under attack, you say "Check!" The owner of the king tries to remove him from attack. If the king cannot escape, he is said to be checkmated and the game is over.

Most games end before a king is checkmated. When the opposing player sees he has no chance to win, he resigns.

Many games end in a draw. Drawn games happen for the following reasons:

1. There aren't enough strong pieces left on the board for either player to force a checkmate.

2. Sometimes the attacking player can only check a king in the same way, over and over. The king will always escape the same way. If an identical check and escape occur three times in a row, with each player making the same move each time, the game is called a draw.

3. A stalemate occurs when a player has a turn but cannot make a legal move even though his king is not in check.

Queening a Pawn. There is an interesting move in chess called "Queening." If a pawn manages to move clear across the board to the first rank on his opponent's side, he can be replaced by a power piece. Usually the player chooses to put another queen on the board, even if he already has one in play. Having two or more queens gives a player a tremendous advantage. It is also exciting to have a small weak piece like a pawn survive all the dangers of the battlefield and be rewarded with power and prestige.

Gambit. I explained the strategy of the gambit on the first page but I'll repeat it here because it played such a big part in what happened with Josie Nolan, Tory Mitchell, and me.

A gambit is a strategy in chess in which a player gives up or sacrifices a game piece in order to get into a better winning position. The most dangerous gambit is a queen's gambit because the queen is the most powerful chess piece. A gambit is a very high-risk play. No player should try it unless he is sure he can live with the way the game turns out.